MW01116391

DEATH OF DREAMS

A Manny Rivera Mystery

Rich Curtin

Cover Design by Berge Design

ISBN-13: 9798332897313

DEATH OF DREAMS

1

DEPUTY SHERIFF MANNY RIVERA had serious doubts about his current assignment as he drove his Sheriff's Department Ford F-150 pickup through Castle Valley toward the LaSal Mountains. It was probably a waste of time, but there was a pleasant upside—it got him out of the office and into the backcountry he loved.

On his left were the red rock pinnacles and buttes that towered majestically over the valley, and on his right were the looming cliff faces of Porcupine Rim. Straight ahead were the peaks of the LaSals, lightly dusted last night with an early-season snowfall. It was mid-September, and the dark blue skies were populated with bright-white cumulus clouds. The air was cool and crystal clear and carried with it the resinous scent of sage.

The beauty of the mountains, mesas, and canyons of Grand County was the thing he loved most about living in Moab. As a deputy, the need to enter the backcountry came often, and he regarded such opportunities as a fringe benefit of his job. He loved the fresh air, the vast vistas, and the silence. He'd never had a desire to serve as a big city cop, surrounded all day by skyscrapers, concrete, and asphalt, even though the pay was substantially higher. Inhaling exhaust fumes from heavy traffic all day long while being subjected to the irritating cacophony of honking horns was not his idea of a desirable work environment. If he had a choice, his love of the high desert would keep him here for the rest of his life.

Rivera and his passenger were responding to an early morning call from Hazel Treadwell who lived alone in a cabin in the mountains. She claimed she had seen a wolf prowling behind her place around sunrise and was afraid for herself and her dogs.

Rivera was pretty sure there were no wolves in the LaSals and hadn't been for a hundred years. A concerted effort by Utah cattle ranchers had long ago wiped them out. The last confirmed wolf sighting in the LaSals had taken place in the 1930s. Nevertheless, he was taking her call seriously because an anonymous rogue group called *Restore the Wolves* had placed a notice in The Times-Independent, Moab's weekly newspaper, stating that they'd released three mated pairs of gray wolves into the LaSals. Their expressed purpose was to help restore the balance of wildlife to the land's original state. The announcement had appeared in the most recent issue of the newspaper.

Until today, no one had reported seeing wolves in the LaSals since the notice was published, so he couldn't be sure if the group's assertion was true or just some kind of hoax. Hoax or not, local cattle ranchers who moved their herds into the mountains during the summer months to take advantage of the fresh grass and good grazing were not amused. Their reactions had ranged from concerned to angry, as the presence of wolves would represent a substantial threat to their cows and calves, and therefore their livelihood.

Before leaving Moab, Rivera had stopped at the Bureau of Land Management Field Office and picked up Ralph Lansing, a young and eager professional with degrees in biology and animal husbandry. He was the BLM's project manager in charge of the mountain goat repopulation program for the LaSal Mountains. Rivera, since he'd never seen a wolf in real life, wanted a wildlife expert to join him on his visit to the Treadwell place. He hoped Lansing could help him confirm or refute Hazel's claim that she had seen a wolf.

For the first half of the drive, Lansing talked about his new girlfriend Veronica. He spoke non-stop, telling Rivera about how attractive she was, how he'd met her, how she wanted him to meet her parents, and his thoughts and fears about getting married. It made Rivera think about his own life, about a couple of relationships that didn't work out for him, about meeting Gloria Valdez during an investigation that took him into the tiny mountain villages of northern New Mexico, and about marrying her and being so thankful he did.

Abruptly, Lansing changed the subject. "Thanks for inviting me to come along, Manny. I hope this wolf report is a false alarm. Wolves in the LaSals would be a real threat to my mountain goats. We relocated thirty-five of them from the Tushar Mountains to the LaSals about ten years ago. Their population has grown to over a hundred now, so they're adapting well. Wolves in the LaSals would completely change the equation, not only for the mountain goats, but also for the bighorn sheep which are undergoing a similar repopulation effort." Lansing thought for a moment, took a sip of coffee from a Styrofoam cup he'd brought along. "You know, back in the 1800s when Utah was still a territory, there was a bounty on wolves. One dollar for each one killed. In those days, that was pretty good money. So, after several decades of hunting down wolves and killing them for profit, there were virtually no wolves left in Utah." Lansing continued on about the threat, telling Rivera things he pretty much already knew.

Now Rivera was only half listening, his mind instead dwelling on the beauty of Castle Valley, how he wished he and Gloria could afford to buy a home out here, and what a wonderful place this would be to someday raise their children. Rivera found himself thinking about children often these days. He grew up in the bosom of a close-knit family in Las Cruces, New Mexico, surrounded by parents, grandparents, brothers, sisters, aunts, uncles, cousins and friends. He looked forward to being reunited with all of them in a couple of weeks when he and Gloria would drive down to Las Cruces for the Rivera family's annual barbeque. That was the kind of family life he longed for. He and his bride had been married for over a year, but as yet there had been no pregnancy. He hoped they would soon be blessed.

Lansing continued voicing his thoughts. "If this wolf sighting business is true, we have another set of issues. As I'm sure you know, wolves are now protected by the Endangered Species Act, so it's illegal to kill them. They will thrive and multiply in the mountains and cause all kinds of havoc. The people who live around here will have to adapt to their presence whether they like it or not. So will the mountain goats, the bighorns, and the cattlemen, I suppose."

Rivera passed through Castle Valley and began ascending the switchbacks of the Castleton-Gateway Road into the mountains. Higher up, they spotted a herd of mule deer, then came upon a striking panoramic view of the Book Cliffs, and beyond them the Roan Cliffs, and farther still, a hundred miles to the north, a dark cloud with spindly bolts of lightning dancing below it. Two miles later, he turned right onto a gravel road and entered an area populated with white-barked aspen trees, their leaves beginning the transformation from green to gold as the nights became cooler. Soon he turned left onto a two-track which led to the Treadwell homestead.

He drove with care on the primitive road, wondering why Hazel had chosen to live out here in relative isolation instead of living in Moab. He'd heard a little bit about her over the years but had never met her. Word had it she was a recluse by choice, and at sixty-seven years of age, she just wanted to be with her dogs and read books. She'd had enough of civilization and the mind-numbing news and disappointments that came with it. She'd been described as crusty, independent, and plain spoken.

The track ended at a small clearing in the woods, about a half-acre in size, with an old log cabin in the center. A maroon, early-model GMC pickup truck covered with dust was parked in front. Aspens, pines, and brush surrounded the clearing, and a carpet of pine needles covered the ground. A garden on the side of the cabin produced a crop of pumpkins, squash, and carrots. It was protected on the sides and top with a barrier of chicken wire. A couple of cords of wood were stacked near the garden. All was quiet except for the rustling of tree branches in the breeze and the squawks of distant pinyon jays echoing in the forest.

Rivera scanned the area as he and Lansing approached the cabin, alert for any sign of a wolf. He knew wolves were ferocious and not to be taken lightly. A woman opened the door just as he started to knock. She was wearing weathered jeans and a faded yellow sweatshirt. She was tan and wrinkled, and her long, gray hair was tied back in a ponytail. There was a look of concern on her face.

"Thanks for coming. I'm Hazel Treadwell. You boys c'mon in. It ain't safe out there."

After the two men stepped into the cabin, she shot a glance outside, then quickly closed the door behind them. Rivera surveyed the interior of the home. It was rustic and warm. The living area had a large stone fireplace and was furnished with a couch and two stuffed armchairs. A framed photograph of an unsmiling elderly man with a long white beard rested on an end table. There were two sets of bookshelves against the far wall. One was crammed with books and magazines and the other displayed an array of family photos.

Rivera introduced himself and his associate. "Are you alright?" he asked.

"I'm fine, except that damn wolf has me worried half to death. I'm afraid for my dogs."

"Do you live here alone?"

"Yes. That's the way I prefer it. My grandfather built this place nearly a century ago. I was raised in Moab but spent every summer up here with Grandpa where it was cooler." She pointed. "That's him in the photograph. I like being here, away from the hordes of tourists in town. My daughter wants me to move in with her in Dallas, but that'll never happen. I want nothing to do with crowds."

"Are the dogs inside now?"

"Of course. They're in the bedroom. When I took them outside a little while ago to do their business, I stood guard with my shotgun."

"What time did you see the animal this morning?" Rivera refrained from using the word wolf because he had no evidence it was a wolf.

"It was about seven o'clock or a little after."

"What made you think it was a wolf? Could it have been a large dog or a coyote? Or maybe a fox?" As soon as the words came out of Rivera's mouth, he knew he'd made a big mistake.

Hazel produced an expression that looked like it was reserved for idiots. She spoke in an indignant tone of voice. "Mister, I've lived in these mountains longer than you've been alive. I sure as hell know what a coyote and a fox look like. And that wasn't no big dog. It was a wolf." She walked to a table, retrieved a digital camera, pressed some buttons, and looked at the screen. "I took two photos of it through the window before it trotted off. Here, take a look. If that's not a wolf, I don't know what is."

Rivera took the camera and studied the image on the screen. The display was small and showed what appeared to be some type of canine peering out from the brush at the edge of the clearing. Rivera couldn't be sure if the animal was a wolf because the screen was so tiny. He showed the image to Lansing who studied it for a moment, then shook his head. "Hard to say. The image is too small."

"Do you have a computer?" asked Rivera. "If we transfer this image to a computer, we can expand it."

She laughed a humorless laugh. "No way. Computers are like televisions. They bring nothing but bad news. And those podcasts are ridiculous. Everybody's got one, and they spend hours spewing their opinions about every damn thing. I'm surprised anyone listens to that garbage."

"I have a laptop in my vehicle." Rivera left the cabin and walked quickly to his pickup while scanning his surroundings. He found himself becoming more and more wary because of all the talk about wolves.

He returned with a laptop and a connecting cable, connected the camera to the laptop, and downloaded the files containing the canine images. He expanded the image and studied it. The animal sure looked like a wolf. It was powerfully built with yellowish eyes, large paws, small triangular-shaped ears, and a strong looking jaw. It had the shaded gray and brown coloring of a wolf. He showed it to Lansing.

Lansing peered at the screen. Nodded. "It's a gray wolf. No question about it."

"There, I told you so," Hazel said. "It wasn't no coyote or fox or big dog. So, what should I do if I see it again? Shoot it with my rifle?"

Lansing answered before Rivera could respond. "Wolves are protected by the Endangered Species Act. Killing a wolf is a felony. I wouldn't recommend it."

She looked at Rivera. "Then what the hell am I supposed to do?"

Rivera thought for a moment. "I'm not sure. If it attacks you or your dogs, I'd say you'd be within your rights to shoot it. If it's just passing through, you should probably leave it alone." Rivera felt stupid for giving such a lame, uninformed answer. He looked at Lansing for help.

Lansing didn't have much to add. "Yeah, I'd say that's the right way to look at it."

Hazel shook her head. "I love my dogs. If I see that wolf prowling around here again, I might just kill the damn thing and bury it," she said, her voice trembling with a mixture of belligerence and fear. "And you know something? No one would know the difference. There's no one living around here but me."

2

AS HE DESCENDED the mountains on the drive back to Moab, Rivera thought about wolves in the LaSals, the danger they posed, and how the community would react when word got out about their newly established presence. Surely Hazel would mention the wolf sighting to her friends. The news would be the number one topic of conversation, spreading quickly throughout Moab and southeast Utah.

By evening, everyone in town would know that the notice published in The Times-Independent by the *Restore the Wolves* group was legitimate and not a hoax. No doubt the newspaper would be publishing follow-on stories, and the radio stations which covered the news would be providing daily updates. The Charlie Abbott Show on Moab's talk radio station would be filled with commentary from listeners calling in to ask questions and give their opinions, pro and con. Rivera retrieved his cell phone and called Millie Ives, the sheriff's dispatcher. He reported to her what he'd learned. At the moment, there was nothing more he could do.

"Thanks for helping me out today, Ralph," said Rivera.

"Any time, Manny," said Lansing. "That Hazel Treadwell was quite a woman, wasn't she?"

"Yeah. She's not afraid to speak her mind. But she has a valid point. What is she supposed to do if that wolf shows up at her place every day looking for a meal? Anyway, that notice published in the newspaper about wolves was obviously no hoax, so now we know there are six wolves roaming the mountains. And as the years roll by, that number will increase."

"The wolves will likely adapt to their new surroundings," said Lansing. "They'll breed and multiply. Someday there will be wolf packs roaming the LaSals. Back in the 1990s, fourteen wolves were captured in Canada and released into Yellowstone. They've adapted well and now there are over a hundred of them in the park. Their presence has altered the entire animal and plant ecosystem. And more recently, there was a sanctioned wolf release in Colorado. Ten gray wolves were relocated from Oregon to the western slope of the Rockies."

"What about the hiking community? Should they be concerned?"

"Not so much. Fatal wolf attacks on human beings are rare. In North America, there were just a couple in the past century." He chuckled. "Maybe we humans don't taste so good."

"What about non-fatal attacks on humans?"

"Around twenty or so in North America during the last century. Of course, with their sharp teeth and powerful jaws, injuries from a wolf attack would be severe. So, not many attacks on humans, but the impact on my mountain goats and the cattle herds could be significant."

Rivera exited the mountains, passed through Castle Valley, and turned left on Hwy 128. The road paralleled the Colorado River as it wound its way toward Moab between massive red rock cliffs. It was one of Rivera's favorite drives. The beauty of the canyon lifted Rivera's spirits, and the unpleasant wolf business began to fade from his thoughts.

His thinking reverted to Gloria and how much he missed her. She was in Phoenix attending the BLM school for newly minted rangers and would be gone for another week. A former deputy sheriff in Rio Arriba County in New Mexico, she was now in training to become a BLM investigative agent. Spending his life with her was the best decision he'd ever made. She was fun and smart and beautiful, the perfect partner on his journey through life. All that was missing in their lives was a newborn baby he could hold in his arms. He felt himself smiling as he thought about the periodic calls from Gloria's mother tactfully inquiring as to whether a grandchild might be on the way. After all, they'd been married a whole year.

As he rounded a curve in the road and crested a hill, the sight of a roadside memorial up ahead interrupted his thoughts and changed his mood. He had seen hundreds of such memorials in New Mexico where he was raised, but the sight of one still had a chilling effect on him. This one reminded him of the senseless death of a nineteen-year-old girl two months ago. The memorial consisted of a wooden cross painted white with a rosary draped around it, an array of multicolored plastic flowers, and a wooden sign with the name Lucia Navarro carved into it. A small, rectangular, white picket fence bordered the memorial.

Rivera noticed the cross was tilted to one side, probably a result of the winds which accompanied the mild cold front that passed through the area last night. He pulled his pickup to a stop on the shoulder of the highway and told Lansing he'd be just a minute. He walked back to the memorial, restored the cross to its upright position, and wedged some additional rocks around its base for sturdier support.

He stood gazing at the memorial, feeling a dispiriting sadness. Lucia had accidentally driven her Jeep off the road one night and plunged forty feet to her death. During the autopsy, blood tests had shown she was under the influence of mescaline, the hallucinogenic drug contained in peyote cactus. In addition, traces of peyote matter were found in her digestive system. A few days after the funeral, her distraught father Emiliano had visited the Grand County Sheriff's Office and asked if they were able to find out where his daughter had gotten the peyote. Unfortunately, an agent of the Drug

Enforcement Administration had earlier contacted the sheriff and instructed her to stay out of the case as it might be related to a larger peyote investigation the DEA was working on. Furthermore, the DEA's involvement was to be kept secret. The sheriff's office complied and was therefore unable to provide Mr. Navarro with any information about the investigation. Worse, they couldn't tell him why.

The father had returned many times, humbly pleading for information like a supplicant, persisting day after day. Rivera could still see the man standing there, big brown eyes, light brown skin, holding his straw hat with both hands as he spoke to the deputy. He was in his mid-forties, a short stocky man with the arms and shoulders of someone who had done physical labor his whole life. A silver cross hung from a chain around his neck.

He'd told Rivera that he'd come to America from Mexico fifteen years ago, originally as a field worker, following the crops in California as they became ripe for harvesting. Then he'd become proficient in carpentry and worked the last eight years on house and condo construction projects in Moab. He said his daughter was smart—much smarter than he was—and that she had received a scholarship to the Utah State University campus in Moab. She was in her junior year working toward a bachelor's degree in business. It was obvious to Rivera how proud he'd been of his daughter.

Mr. Navarro's visits had become less frequent in the past two weeks, finally tapering off altogether. Perhaps, thought Rivera, he'd resigned himself to never learning where Lucia had gotten the peyote, and simply accepted the loss that fate had dealt him. Perhaps he'd found sanctuary in his religious beliefs. Or perhaps he figured it didn't matter now anyway. Lucia was gone.

Rivera had spoken to him during most of his visits and listened to his pleas but could only offer sympathy. In his gut, the deputy was deeply troubled by his inability to help the bereaved father, or at least tell him that the DEA was investigating the matter. He resented being muzzled this way and wished he could find a way to help the man. He shook his head in disgust.

Rivera had thought several times about breaking the rules and confiding in the man, but he had no desire to undermine an ongoing DEA investigation. Then he thought about how he would react if it were his child who had been killed because of a drug overdose. With anguish and unbridled anger, he imagined. It occurred to him that having children wasn't without risk. Significant risk. He took one last look at the roadside memorial, returned to his vehicle, and resumed his trip to Moab in silence.

Rivera turned left at Main Street and headed into town. The streets were crowded and the traffic was stop and go. He reflected on the town's growth as he sat there waiting for the traffic to move. Moab had come a long way since it was just a tiny settlement on the Old Spanish

Trail, a stopping off point before crossing the Colorado River. From those humble beginnings, it became a boom town in the 1950s when uranium was discovered in southeast Utah and prospectors flocked to the area in search of wealth. Years later, the demand for uranium subsided, and the town fell on hard times. It languished for several years, then was rejuvenated as word of the red rock backcountry and its beauty spread throughout the adventure seeking world, causing an influx of visitors and permanent residents.

Just as he passed through the center of town, his cell phone buzzed. It was Millie Ives. "Manny, we have a reported shooting up in the LaSals. A man named Peter Simpson called it in. He and his brother Ronnie were up there hunting elk. He said the victim had what looked like a bullet wound in the back. They checked him for a pulse, and Peter, who's an Emergency Medical Technician from Moab, said he was certain the man was dead. The brothers were acquainted with the victim—his name is Derek Webster. Location is at the end of a two track that heads north off Warner Lake Road. It dead ends after about a quarter mile at Wilcox Flat. The site overlooks Spring Creek Canyon." She gave Rivera the GPS coordinates.

"Okay, Millie, I'm on my way."

Rivera drove three blocks to the BLM Field Office, dropped Lansing off, switched on his light bar, and sped south out of town. Rivera knew Warner Lake Road well,

17

as he and Gloria had driven to the lake several times, once for a picnic with friends and several times just to set out a couple of lawn chairs and relax. As he drove, he wondered if the shooting was accidental—there were a lot of hunters in the mountains this time of year.

He drove through Spanish Valley and turned onto the LaSal Mountain Loop Road, following its twists and turns as it climbed to higher altitudes. He turned right onto the road leading to Warner Lake and continued still higher into the mountains. A half mile before reaching the lake, he spotted a two-track heading north. He stopped, checked his GPS receiver, decided that was the correct road, and turned left.

The road was primitive and rugged. Rivera gripped the steering wheel tightly as his pickup bumped and jolted ahead through the coniferous forest. A half mile later, the road ended at a small clearing overlooking a shallow canyon. Rivera stopped and scanned the area.

Parked ahead were a dark green Toyota pickup and a silver Ford Bronco Raptor with a high clearance suspension. The Raptor's engine was idling, and its rear door was swung open to the side. Mounted in the bed were two side-by-side equipment racks filled with what appeared to be expensive electronic instruments. The instruments were facing rearward toward a man seated in an orange canvas chair. His body was slumped forward and there was a bloody spot on the back of his bright orange vest.

Two men were standing next to the Toyota pickup, staring wide-eyed at Rivera. They appeared shaken and relieved to see him. One of them raised his hand in a half-hearted wave. It was then that Rivera recognized them. Although he'd never met them, he'd seen them in church a few times.

3

RIVERA NODDED TOWARD the two men and approached the Raptor. The victim's head was turned to one side and rested on the bed of the vehicle. He was a handsome fellow and looked to be in his late thirties or early forties. He had a ruddy complexion, a three-day stubble, and a full head of brown wavy hair. Rivera pressed his fingers against the man's carotid artery and checked for a pulse. He found none. He checked a second time and got the same result. During his law enforcement career, he had seen the corpses of many people dead before their time, some killed intentionally and some accidentally. He was well beyond being shocked at the sight, but each time he was left with the same empty feeling—another life wasted, another distraught family.

He called the dispatcher, reported the situation, and requested she send the Medical Examiner. Then he turned his attention to the two men waiting by the Toyota. Both were tall and lanky and wore jeans, flannel shirts, bright orange vests, and orange baseball caps. One appeared to be in his thirties and had auburn hair. The other was younger with shoulder-length blond hair.

The older one, who was holding a satellite phone, stepped forward. "Deputy, I'm Peter Simpson and this is my brother Ronnie," he said in a soft voice. Then he gestured toward the man in the chair. "That's Derek Webster. We found him sitting there just like that. I checked and couldn't find a pulse. It looks like he caught a bullet in the back. We figured it was probably an errant shot from some hunter's rifle. It's hunting season, so there are lots of hunters up here in the mountains. We called it in right away."

"The dispatcher said you were up here hunting elk." Rivera left it as a question.

"That's right," said the elder brother.

Rivera scanned the area and saw no weapons. "Where are your rifles?"

"No rifles. We're bow hunters. We put our equipment back in my truck. The season for bow hunting ends the day after tomorrow. The rifle season lasts a lot longer. We've had no luck so far. I have a rock fireplace in my den with an open space above it, just waiting for a fine set of antlers to be mounted there.

Rivera wondered how the fellow's attention could be focused on antlers with a dead man sitting not thirty feet away. He jotted their names, addresses, and phone numbers into his notepad and instructed them to wait by his vehicle. Then he turned his attention to the victim.

He took a close look at the bullet wound in the center of the man's back. It appeared that the bullet had passed through the back of the canvas chair before entering the victim. Rivera figured he was working with the electronics gear in the truck when he was shot. A satellite phone lay on the ground at the victim's feet.

As Rivera inspected the body from head to toe, he saw something that surprised him. The spaces between the man's pants cuffs and his shoes revealed that he had prosthetic feet.

Rivera studied the two racks filled with electronic equipment. He didn't recognize any of the devices, except for a couple of color monitors and a computer keyboard. He judged that the monitors would have been at eye level with the victim, had he been sitting upright in his chair. The monitor on the right displayed a frozen image of what appeared to be typical mesa terrain. The one on the left displayed a topographic map of a portion of the LaSals, a red dot highlighting a particular location.

Rivera extracted the victim's wallet from his pocket and pulled out his driver's license. Derek Webster lived in Moab, a half dozen blocks from the house Rivera rented. He was forty-two-years old, just a couple of years older than Rivera. The deputy strung yellow crime scene tape around the area and turned his attention to the Simpson brothers.

"Tell me why you happened to be at this particular location today."

The older brother responded. "As I said, we're bow hunters. We have elk permits and were hoping to score a bull elk with a large rack of antlers before the bow season ended. We've tried for the past few years to get one but haven't had any luck. Just a lot of hiking through the woods with no results. We'd heard from a fellow hunter named Billy Blevins that Derek could help, so we hired him to find us an elk."

"Is that what all that electronic equipment is for?"

"Right. Derek's a drone expert. He was using his drone to search for a bull elk. The drone does most of the legwork for us hunters. Derek transmits control signals to the drone's main receiver to direct its path. Besides the main receiver, there's also a GPS receiver, a video camera, and a transmitter on board. The transmitter sends a video image of what the camera sees back to the receiver in the truck along with the drone's GPS coordinates."

"You mean he sits here exploring for a suitable animal and tells you which way to go to find it?"

"Exactly. The drone can explore the backcountry much faster than we can on foot. So after the launch, we all watched the video image on the large color monitor. When Derek located a herd and we identified the animal we wanted, he gave us the GPS coordinates, and off we went. As we hiked, he communicated with us by satellite phone and told us the best route to take." He handed Rivera the satellite phone he was holding. "Derek loaned us this satellite phone to take with us on our hike. When the elk changed its location, Derek called us with the new coordinates and communicated any adjustment in the route. The smaller monitor displays a topo map of the area. The red dot on the map shows the location of the drone. It's all pretty cool."

Rivera had never heard of hunting this way. It seemed a bit unfair to him, but that was none of his business. He pulled out his pen and notepad from his shirt pocket. "So, what happened this morning? How did all this unfold?"

"We hired Derek for today. We wanted…"

"Hold on. When did you hire him?"

"About a week ago. We'd heard good things about his services and decided to give high-tech hunting a try. It was expensive—six hundred for the day—but we figured it would save a lot of legwork. And we badly wanted a set of trophy antlers. With the bow season about to expire, we were getting kind of desperate."

"You said you have a bow license?"

"Right. We each have one." They showed Rivera their licenses. "We met Derek in town early this morning and followed him out here. He knew the mountains real well and said this spot would be a good place to start looking. We waited while he set up his equipment. Then he launched the drone and sent it off on a short test run to make sure everything was operating properly. The drone returned from the test, and Derek said all the controls checked out, so he sent it off on its search for a bull. The three of us watched the monitor as he explored the area east of here. After twenty minutes or so, he spotted a small herd of elk on the west slope of Mount Waas. There was a bull among them with a huge rack. We jumped for joy and told Derek that's the one for us. He gave us the GPS coordinates and pointed out the best route on the monitor. Off we went."

"What time was that?"

"About nine o'clock. Since the herd was moving, Derek continually sent us updates on its location, and we adjusted our route accordingly. After about forty-five minutes, Derek said we were getting close. 'Keep heading east,' he said. Then the transmissions stopped. We kept trying to contact him, but there was no response. We looked for the herd for a while but had no luck. Without Derek's guidance, we were lost. We decided to head back. We retraced the waypoints stored in our GPS receiver and returned here, where we started." He pointed without looking. "And we found Derek...like that and called the sheriff's office."

"Did you hear any gunshots this morning?'

"Yeah, a few. I'm sure there are other hunters in the area today."

Rivera knew that had to be correct. This time of year was prime elk hunting season, and the LaSal Mountains were a popular spot for hunters from Utah and Colorado.

"I noticed he has prosthetic feet."

"Yeah. Billy Blevins told us about that. He said Derek lost everything from his calves on down in some kind of auto accident."

Rivera jotted that detail into his notepad and decided he had all the information he needed from the hunters for now. He thanked them and told them they were free to go. He walked with them to their truck and glanced through the window to verify there were no guns inside. He saw two expensive compound bows, two quivers filled with carbon arrows, and a couple of day packs.

As they opened the doors to get into the truck, the younger brother hesitated. "What about our money? We gave him six hundred dollars this morning. He put it in his shirt pocket. Can I go get it back? I won't touch anything else."

"Never mind that," said the older brother in a stern tone of voice. "The poor guy's dead."

4

RIVERA RETURNED TO the Raptor to make a closer inspection of its contents. Besides the racks of electronic equipment, there wasn't much else of significance. Just strategically located grab bars to assist in getting in and out, a toolbox, a spare drone, some clothing, and a day pack filled with snacks and bottles of water.

He checked the glove box and found the usual contents—proof of insurance, oil change receipts, a tire pressure gauge, and an operator's manual for the vehicle. The center console contained a cell phone, maps of the Four Corners area, a collection of country and western CDs, a pair of expensive binoculars, a ballpoint pen, and a pair of sunglasses in a case. A cup half-filled with coffee, now cold, rested in a cupholder. Nothing unusual.

The Raptor was expensive. The tires alone had to be worth five hundred dollars apiece. Horizontal scratch marks on the sides of the Raptor were typical for a backcountry vehicle, the result of driving on narrow dirt roads with the stiff branches of black brush and sage encroaching on each side.

He wondered about Derek Webster. It seemed odd for a man with prosthetic feet to be active in the backcountry. But Derek had found a way. He was able to drive to this remote location, open the rear door of the Raptor, place a canvas chair outside, climb into it, launch a drone, and operate the equipment mounted in the vehicle. He could remain stationary and explore the backcountry at the same time. Impressive. Maybe even heroic. And it appeared he was able to derive some income from the setup.

Rivera wondered if Derek had any family in town. He extracted his cell phone and called Chris Carey, a close friend who lived in Moab. Carey was a retired investigative journalist who had worked for several Utah newspapers and was regarded as one of the best in his field. Then, as news channels, websites, and podcasts proliferated and became more and more accepted by the general public, layoffs in the newspaper industry began. As Carey had explained it, each newspaper, one by one, had significantly reduced its senior staff and had pretty much abandoned any pretense of serving the people as an investigative medium. That was the end of Carey's stellar career. Now, with his investigative chops still intact and strong, he was always an eager collaborator whenever Rivera needed information on the history or the residents of Grand County. Carey could be trusted to work confidentially and loved to get involved with Rivera's cases. It helped feed his need for investigative challenges. Despite their age difference—Carey was in his early seventies and Rivera had just turned forty— they had become close friends.

"Hi, Manny. Great to hear from you." There was a note of enthusiasm in his voice.

"Chris, I'm in the LaSals at the scene of a shooting and I need some help identifying the victim's family. Do you know a man named Derek Webster from Moab?"

"I don't know him personally, but I heard a little about him years ago from his father Harold. The father, who goes by Hal, owns that wholesale nursery operation on the river just across the Dewey Bridge. He's had that place for over thirty years. You've probably driven past it a hundred times."

"Yes, I know where you mean. What did you learn about Derek from his father?"

"I visited the nursery a few times as part of a story I was writing about small businesses in Grand County. This was about six years ago. The father and I were chatting one time, and I remember him telling me a little about his son. I could tell he was very proud of him. Hal said Derek had been an avid hiker in the Four Corners area for years. He knew the backcountry as well as anyone. Mostly solo stuff, but sometimes outfitters would hire him to lead trail hikes for groups. As I understand it, he was one of the best. He lived for exploring the canyons, mesas, and mountains. It was his whole life. He did a lot of rafting too. He ran the rapids of Cataract Canyon on a regular basis. I remember thinking I should write an article about Derek and like-minded individuals who spend their lives exploring the backcountry. You know, why they did it, what it felt like to be alone in the wilderness for weeks at a time, and what staring at the starry skies night after night caused them to think about. Years later, I heard Derek was involved in some kind of automobile accident where he lost the use of his feet, but I don't have any details on that."

"Okay, thanks, Chris."

"If there's anything I can do to help, just let me know," said Carey with a hopeful note in his voice. "You know how much I enjoy helping you on your cases."

"Will do, Chris. Thank you."

Rivera knew that after he was through at the crime scene, it would be his unpleasant duty to visit Derek's father and give him the bad news. That was the part of his job that he dreaded. Delivering spirit-crushing news to a family about the death of a loved one was always difficult for him. The resulting discomfort hung with him for weeks afterwards. It was almost like a feeling of guilt, as though he were partially responsible for their grief.

Rivera wondered if Derek's death was due to a stray bullet from a hunter's rifle or something more sinister. After giving it some thought, he concluded the shooting was most likely intentional. There was no proof, of course, but Derek was wearing a bright orange vest for safety, yet the bullet struck him squarely in the center of the back.

Even his chair was bright orange. A hunter would not mistake an orange target for an elk or a deer. Clearly, if the bullet had been fired from nearby, the shooter would have seen the orange clothing and the two vehicles. But suppose the bullet had been fired from a great distance. A bullet fired from a 30-06 rifle can travel well over a mile. In that case, though, it would have to penetrate the walls of the thick pine forest that surrounded the small clearing where Derek had parked, a highly improbable likelihood in Rivera's mind. His instincts told him he was dealing with a murder case. Until he learned otherwise, he would proceed on the basis of that assumption.

Rivera thought through the sequence of events based upon what he had learned thus far. Derek had gotten up early, met with the bow hunters somewhere in town, and driven up here. Then he set up his equipment, launched a drone, located an elk herd, and found within it a bull with an exceptional rack. The hunters indicated that animal was the one they wanted. Derek sent the hunters on their way, keeping track of the bull's movements, and providing periodic route updates to the hunters. Simultaneously, the hunters kept Derek apprised of their position via satellite phone. At some point during that sequence of events, a bullet struck Derek squarely in the back and killed him. When Derek's communications with the hunters ended, they decided to return. Upon finding Derek shot dead, they called the sheriff's office.

Rivera took photographs of the general area and close-ups of the victim, his wound, and the van. Then he emptied Derek's pants pockets and placed each item into an evidence bag. Nothing struck him as unusual. There was a wallet which contained a driver's license, some credit cards, and forty-four dollars in cash. Also some coins, a keyring with four keys, a vehicle key fob, and a handkerchief. In the victim's shirt pocket, he found six one-hundred-dollar bills, obviously the money the Simpson brothers had paid him for his services.

He glanced at the racks of electronic equipment in the van, puzzled by the complex system with its intricate switches, knobs, indicator lights, and displays. He decided that he needed expert help to understand how everything worked. A visit to Charlie Savage, his go-to friend for all things technical, would achieve that objective. It occurred to Rivera that somewhere in the wilderness, the drone was still out there lying on the ground, its batteries having by now expended all their stored energy.

A half-hour later, Dr. Marvin Phelps, the County Medical Examiner, arrived at the scene in his pickup truck. He was a slender man in his thirties with wavy brown hair framing a boyish face. He exchanged greetings with Rivera and walked directly to the corpse. He studied the body for a brief period, checked the carotid artery, checked the victim's eyes, looked in his mouth, touched the back wound, checked the chest for an exit wound, inspected the prostheses, and shook his head.

"Let's get him to the hospital morgue, and I'll do a complete autopsy. But I'd say the cause of death is likely the obvious—a bullet in the back. Probably penetrated his heart."

"Okay, Marvin, I'll have him picked up and delivered to the hospital. How soon can you perform an autopsy?"

"I'll wait at the hospital and get on it as soon as he arrives."

"Great. Thanks."

After Phelps departed, a vehicle from the mortuary arrived and two men picked up the body for transport to the morgue. Soon thereafter, two deputies arrived to transport Derek's Bronco Raptor to the sheriff's impound lot. One hopped out, got the key fob for the Raptor from Rivera, and packed the two satellite phones and the canvas chair into the vehicle. He closed the rear door and hoisted himself into the van. Then they departed, leaving Rivera there by himself. Nothing was left now but the yellow crime scene tape rippling in the breeze.

It was late afternoon, and the sun was low in the western sky. Three ravens circled high in the sky, appearing as black specks against a large cumulus cloud. Cold air had started drifting down the mountain slopes, giving him a shiver. He stood there looking at the tape and reflecting on this unlikely place for Derek's life to have come to an end. He wondered who stood to benefit from the death of this intrepid soul.

As he walked to his vehicle thinking about his impending meeting with the victim's father, the risks of having children of his own again entered his mind. This was yet another example of what could go wrong in an otherwise happy family. What if someday an officer were on his way to Rivera's home to give him the bad news about the death of his child? Rivera quickly forced that thought out of his mind. He got into his truck and headed for the Webster Nursery.

5

RIVERA DESCENDED FROM the mountains and drove through Castle Valley. He turned right on Hwy 128 and drove twenty miles through scenic red rock canyons, crossing the Dewey Bridge at the Colorado River. A quarter mile beyond the bridge, he saw the entrance to Harold Webster's nursery on the right. A large sign with green letters on a white background read *Webster Wholesale Plant and Tree Nursery.* Rivera had driven past it many times but never had occasion to visit.

He turned on a gravel entry road and drove into the property. The nursery was expansive—he estimated its size at a hundred acres. It was well maintained, and its setting right next to the river gave it not only a source of irrigation water for growing trees and plants, but also a picture postcard look. There were groves of young peach, pecan, desert willow, and other types of trees on the right side of the entry road. Straight ahead was a rock house with a wooden porch in front. It sat near the river snuggled among a half-dozen stately cottonwood trees. To his left was an equipment barn, its open doors exposing endless stacks of plastic pots, a John Deere tractor, and a forklift. Beyond that were three huge greenhouses and a cabin constructed of debarked spruce logs. At the end of the property were fields of green bushes and rows of multicolored flowering plants. Upriver, he could see the confluence of the Dolores and Colorado Rivers, and in the distance were the cliffs of Hotel Mesa. Beyond that was the remote and vast wilderness of an area called the Big Triangle.

A dark green delivery truck was parked near the greenhouses. On its door Rivera could see the words *Webster Nursery* and a stylized image of a pinyon pine. A man was removing wooden crates from the nearest greenhouse and loading them into the back of the truck. The crates were filled with potted orchids and poinsettias. Rivera pulled up next to the truck and opened his window. The man, who looked to be in his early thirties, finished loading a crate onto the truck and approached Rivera with a look of curiosity on his face. He was wearing jeans and a faded blue work shirt. The deputy knew he was too young to be Harold Webster and had to be an employee.

"Can I help you, Deputy?" he asked.

"I'm looking for Mr. Harold Webster."

"I'm Guy Richardson, the manager here. I believe Hal's in the house. Can I get him for you?"

"No, that's all right. I'll just drive over there and knock on the door."

Richardson seemed to be studying Rivera's face. "Is everything okay?"

"I'm afraid I've got some real bad news for him."

Richardson raised his eyebrows. "What kind of bad news?"

"His son Derek was shot and killed this morning."

Richardson's jaw fell open. He took a step back. "What in God's name happened?"

"While he was up in the mountains helping some hunters stalk a bull elk, he was shot in the back. Could have been a hunting accident. It's too soon to know for sure." Rivera saw no point in revealing his strong suspicion that the shooting was deliberate.

Richardson slowly shook his head and remained silent for a long moment. "Hal will be crushed."

"Are there any other family members?"

"Derek was the only family Hal had left. Hal told me once that Derek's birth had been difficult, and Harriet, Hal's wife, was unable to have any more children. Then, a couple of years ago, she passed away."

"I'm gonna head over to the house now and tell him about his son."

"Do you want me to come with you?"

"Maybe you should wait here. But after I leave, he's going to need someone."

"I've worked here since I was sixteen years old. In some ways, he's like a father to me. With Derek gone,

I'm the closest thing he's got to family now. I'll look after him and help him all I can."

Rivera walked to the house. He dreaded what he was about to do. His mentor and first boss, Sheriff Leroy Bradshaw, had told him there's nothing you can do to lessen their pain. Don't beat around the bush. Just tell them as gently and directly as you can.

Rivera girded himself and knocked on the door. An elderly man who appeared to be in his seventies pulled open the door and smiled. He was slender, gray, and stooped, and moved as though his joints were afflicted with arthritis. When he saw the expression on Rivera's face, his smile faded.

"Yessir, Deputy."

"Mr. Harold Webster?"

"Yes."

"I'm afraid I have some terrible news." He hesitated a beat. "Your son Derek was shot and killed in the LaSals this morning."

The old man stared at Rivera with a frozen expression. He reached up for the door jamb to steady himself. "My Derek is dead, you say?"

"Yes. I'm so sorry."

The man stepped out onto the porch and lowered himself into a wicker rocking chair. His eyes welled up with tears. He leaned forward, forearms on knees, and stared at the floor, quivering. He said nothing for a full minute. Then he spoke.

"Why was he shot? Was it an accident?"

"We don't know yet. We'll begin an investigation and inform you as soon as we know."

"Where's my boy now?"

"At the hospital morgue in Moab. An autopsy will be performed shortly."

"After all Derek's been through with the accident and the amputations, then this has to happen. That poor boy." The man shook his head and began sobbing.

Rivera sat down in an adjacent chair and waited there long enough to make sure the man didn't need medical attention. Then he handed him a business card. "Sir, please call me if you need help."

Webster took the card and nodded.

Rivera returned to his vehicle where Richardson was waiting for him.

"I told him," said Rivera. "Needless to say, he's extremely upset."

"I'd better go look after him," said Richardson.

"Before you go, what can you tell me about Derek's accident?"

"As I understand it, he was driving his pickup on Interstate 70 east of Grand Junction. The road was icy, and he got into a bad accident involving an out-of-control eighteen-wheeler and three automobiles. Both of Derek's feet and lower shins were crushed, and he had lots of other injuries too. His legs were amputated somewhere above the ankles."

"Damn shame."

"Yeah. Before the accident, Derek was a dedicated backcountry guy. He loved to hike and camp out. It was his life. He probably hiked every canyon in southeast Utah, some of it requiring technical climbing. After the accident, he was patched up and fitted with prosthetic feet. Eventually, he was able to walk on flat surfaces, but his hiking days were over. He tried working here at the nursery, but the chores we normally do require strength and agility—planting, harvesting, and so forth. Derek gave it his all, but it was no use. He kept falling and injuring himself. After that, he started hitting the bottle pretty hard. He went into a tailspin that lasted a couple of years. His mother—a fine woman, a saint, bless her soul— helped him quit drinking through love and attention. Then, one day he heard about drones and got all excited. I don't understand how the technology works, but the drones allowed him to explore the canyons and mountains, at least in a virtual sense. They partially restored his adventuresome life, enough so that his bond with the wilderness remained intact. He regularly went by himself into the backcountry and launched the drones into places he wanted to explore. That's pretty much all I know about the injury."

"Did he have any close friends?"

Richardson thought for a moment. "Derek started dating a lady earlier this year. Her name is Evelyn Ellwood. Lives in Moab. Nice person. I know Hal was hoping they would get married and have kids so he could someday play with the grandkids." Richardson looked down and kicked a small rock across the yard. "I'd better go look after Hal now."

Rivera gave Richardson one of his cards and received one of Richardson's in return. "I'll be back for another visit in the future. Meanwhile, call me if you think of anything that will help."

As Rivera slowly drove off the property, he glanced in his rear-view mirror. Richardson and Mr. Webster were standing on the porch hugging each other. Rivera inhaled a deep breath, let it out, and headed back to the office.

6

BACK IN MOAB, Rivera parked in front of the sheriff's building and entered. He grabbed a mug of coffee in the break room, headed down the hallway to his office, then stopped. He'd seen one doughnut remaining in the box of a dozen that some good soul had bought and placed there this morning. It would be getting stale by now, but he was hungry. He'd eaten breakfast at the Rim Rock Diner but all he'd had for lunch was a couple of granola bars he kept in his truck for emergencies like today when he was stuck in some remote location for most of the day. Granola bars were no substitute for a real meal. He returned to the break room, retrieved the doughnut, and ate it, washing it down with coffee. That helped, but he was still hungry.

On his desk was a pink *While You Were Out* slip stating that Sheriff Louise Anderson wanted to see him as soon as he returned. He walked down the hall to her office, knocked on the open door, and sat down in one of the padded chairs in front of her walnut desk.

She closed the file she was reading, placed it on her desk, and studied Rivera through rose-rimmed designer glasses. She was in her mid-fifties, tall and slender, and had been divorced for several years. She'd been elected sheriff after serving in the Army for twenty-six years, attaining the rank of colonel. She'd spent most of her career in Military Police administrative jobs. As a newly elected sheriff, her military bearing had carried over and was reflected in her manner. The years mellowed her, as did Moab, and soon she carried herself more like a small-town sheriff than a spit-and-polish colonel. Today, she looked even more relaxed to Rivera. Her make-up had been carefully applied, her eyes looked larger, and she had let her short brown hair grow to shoulder length. Instead of looking like an intense woman with sharp features who was all business, she looked, well, pretty. Rivera wondered if the whispers were true. Had she found herself a secret boyfriend?

"Tell me about the shooting in the mountains," she said.

Rivera briefed her on Derek Webster's drone-for-hire business, his history, and the nature of his handicap. He covered the bow hunters' quest for a trophy bull elk, then summarized the events leading up to the shooting. He related what he had found at the crime scene and the details of his visit to the Webster Nursery. "I'm not *certain* whether it's a murder case or a hunting accident. The mountains are full of hunters this time of year, but a hunting accident seems highly improbable to me. Of all the places a stray bullet could land, this one ends up dead center in Webster's back. Seems like his bright orange vest and the two vehicles parked nearby would have caught the eye of a hunter."

"Sounds right." She sat back and thought for a long moment. "Derek Webster must have been an interesting fellow. He was able to find a way to keep exploring the canyons, even after he lost his legs. That's impressive. A great example of overcoming adversity."

"I think those drones of his must have saved his mental health. They kept his life interesting. After the accident, he had a problem with alcohol that lasted a couple of years, but he beat that and went on to have what sounds like an enjoyable and interesting life, despite his handicap."

"So what's your next step?"

"Learn all I can about him. See if there's a reason someone would want him dead."

"Okay, let me know if you need any help. Now, what about this wolf sighting business?"

"The notice posted in the newspaper from the *Restore the Wolves* group was legit. Hazel Treadwell, who lives in an old cabin in the mountains, saw one behind her house this morning and took photos of it. Ralph Lansing of the BLM confirmed that it was a wolf."

Anderson sat back in her chair. "Now we'll have a whole new set of problems to worry about. Everyone in the county will be buzzing about wolves. Hikers will start carrying firearms for safety. And there's going to be renewed friction between the environmental activists and the ranchers." She shook her head. "Oh well, one day at a time. Keep me posted on the Webster case."

Rivera got up, headed for the door, then stopped. "Have we heard anything more from the DEA on that peyote business?"

"Not a word."

"Why not? Why can't those people at least keep us informed? Is that asking too much?" Rivera felt a familiar irritation rising within him. This wasn't the first time he'd experienced the feds withholding important information regarding a Grand County case. Surely they could give him something he could pass on to Lucia's aggrieved father so the man could believe that he and his daughter mattered.

"I understand your concern." The sheriff spoke in a calm and deliberate voice. "It's officially none of our business. We are to stay out of it." She emphasized the words, *stay out of it*. "I know you've gotten crossways with the DEA before. Do you remember Agent Bill Masters?"

Rivera remembered. It was nine years ago when he was investigating a murder related to a highly organized and well-equipped gang of drug pushers who were growing marijuana on remote plots of BLM land. Masters was in charge of the DEA's investigation, and Rivera was investigating a murder which took place in

Grand County. The trajectories of the two investigations crisscrossed, leading to a high friction situation between the two men.

"I remember him."

"Well, he's the one in charge of the peyote investigation." She peered over her glasses and smiled. "Need I say more?"

"No need. I understand."

Rivera returned to his office, closed the door, and sat down at his desk. He did his best to force the Bill Masters business out of his mind, but it hung with him. Masters was a pushy bureaucrat and a high-level incompetent. Rivera hoped never to see him again, but, oddly, Masters's involvement in the peyote case made the whole matter even more interesting. He found himself motivated to learn more about peyote use in general and particularly in southeast Utah. The research would all have to be done sub rosa, of course.

He took a couple of sips of coffee then leaned back, hoisted his feet onto his desk, and stared out the window at the LaSal Mountains. He liked his office. It was small but comfortable. There was a gray metal desk, a padded chair that swiveled and reclined, a set of bookshelves, and two chairs for visitors. Years ago, he was offered a larger office but declined because he would have lost his view of the mountains. He believed the view helped him relax his mind and think more clearly. And it kept him attached to the backcountry he loved when he was stuck working in the office.

He glanced over at the framed photographs on the bookshelf. There were pictures of his parents, his grandparents, his two brothers and two sisters, and his beloved Gloria. Next to the photographs was an ancient-Indian pot he'd received as a gift from the foreman of the Rutherford Ranch, a pleasant reminder of the first case he'd been assigned as an investigator. He looked at the photograph of his grandfather, the wisest man he ever knew, and was thankful for having him in his life. He was the person Rivera went to for advice on matters of ethics and fairness, and who engrained in the deputy's value system the idea that justice is more important than the letter of the law. Rivera had followed that precept since the beginning of his investigative career. Glancing at those photos always gave him a warm feeling.

Rivera returned his gaze to the mountains. Dusk had set in, and the fading rays of the setting sun reflected off the clouds in the western sky, casting a pink hue on the LaSal peaks. He sat there staring at it, taking a few minutes to unwind from the unpleasant duties of the day. He wanted to forget the difficult meeting he had with Hal Webster and wished there was a way to banish it from his memory.

After a few minutes, he lowered his feet, faced his computer, and turned it on. He checked the Simpson brothers for wants and warrants. They were clean. As an afterthought, he checked Guy Richardson, Mr. Webster's nursery manager. He too was clean. Then he typed up his report outlining what he had learned thus far in the case. Next, he placed the evidence bags containing Derek's items into the evidence locker and logged them in. He decided the bag containing the six hundred dollars he found in Derek's shirt pocket should be returned to the Simpson brothers after the case was closed.

Rivera was tired. Normally he'd be looking forward to spending a relaxing evening with Gloria, but tonight that was not to be. He decided to call it a day, go home, and feed Bentley, his chocolate Labrador retriever who would be eagerly waiting for him in the backyard. Next in line for food would be the fancy guppies that inhabited the ten-gallon aquarium on his kitchen counter. They would be waiting for him, clustered in the corner of the tank closest to him, dancing around and eagerly wagging their colorful tails, reminding him it was dinner time. A pinch of tropical fish food would set them in motion, foraging for each morsel. Finally, he would see to his own needs. He would put a frozen chicken pot pie in the oven for his dinner and later have a beer or two. It was a repeat of the coming-home ritual he followed when he was a single man. He much preferred a home-cooked dinner with Gloria, chatting about the events of the day and making plans for their future. He would call her later in the evening and catch up. And tomorrow, he would visit

Derek Webster's home and start learning everything he could about the man.

7

RIVERA PULLED INTO the parking lot of the Rim Rock Diner. It was early and still dark outside, and there was a chill in the air. He was hungry and eager to get a good breakfast into his stomach. He parked, headed for the entrance, and pulled open the door. The smell of bacon and pancakes cooking on the grill made him salivate. He was greeted by the friendly sounds of locals enjoying each other's company. He waved to the regulars he saw each day including the three octogenarian prospectors who were there each morning recounting tales of the uranium boom of the 1950s. He headed for his usual booth by the window. Emmett Mitchell, his close friend and a deputy sheriff from San Juan County to the south, was waiting for him there. Like Rivera, Mitchell was the lead criminal investigator for his county.

Rivera slid into the booth. "Morning, Emmett." Mitchell was in his early fifties with a pleasant face and dark brown hair, now showing a hint of gray around the temples.

"Look at that," said Mitchell, nodding toward the window.

Rivera looked out the window at the LaSal Mountains on the eastern horizon and saw one of his favorite sights. The sky was dark, and the mountains were backlighted by the rising sun, creating an ethereal orange aura which outlined the black peaks. On Main Street, pickups and Jeeps loaded with adventure seekers were heading out to the backcountry for a day of hiking, exploring, and seeing some of the earth's most incredible red rock scenery.

"Amazing, isn't it?" said Rivera.

"Yeah. I feel lucky to be living here."

Rivera met Mitchell for breakfast at the Rim Rock Diner whenever their schedules permitted. They had grown close over the years. Mitchell had been one of Rivera's mentors in his early days as a deputy and later served as Best Man at Rivera's wedding. They usually chatted about family matters and then got around to sharing the details of the cases they were working on. Today was no exception. In a low voice, Rivera briefed Mitchell on the details of the Webster case.

"He was shot in the back for no obvious reason," Rivera concluded. "Could be a hunting accident, but I have strong doubts."

"What a shame. I remember that guy. I met him once a little over a year ago. We were working with the Search and Rescue people trying to find a little six-year-old girl who got lost in the mountains. A bunch of locals had organized a picnic at LaSal Pass right near Medicine Lake. About sixty people were there. It was a high school graduation celebration. The girl, I remember her name was Melody, wandered off and got lost in the woods. Last anyone saw, she was playing with the other kids. Then she was gone. It was late afternoon and several of us deputies went up there to help the SAR people search for her. It was starting to get dark, and her parents were frantic. Combing the forest with flashlights would make for a difficult search, but that looked like it was going to be our only option."

"So what happened?"

"All of a sudden, this guy pulls up in a Bronco Raptor. One of the SAR people had called him in to help. It was your guy, Derek Webster. The SAR people said they'd used him once before to help in one of their searches. He had prosthetic feet. He dragged a chair to the back of the vehicle, opened the rear door, and sat down in front of a bunch of electronic gear. After some preparatory work, he launched a drone. He told us it was equipped with a night-vision infrared camera and could see images in the dark. It was amazing. He located the girl in less than twenty minutes. She was in the woods asleep on a bed of pine needles, unafraid and unharmed."

"That's impressive. Yesterday, he was helping some bow hunters who had hired him to find a trophy bull elk. Apparently he'd found a way to lead a productive life despite his disability."

Betty, a waitress at the Rim Rock Diner for longer than Rivera had lived in Moab, came to their table with a carafe of coffee and two mugs. She leaned forward and filled the mugs. She was fifty something and heavily made up, with long blonde hair piled haphazardly on top of her head. As usual, the top three buttons of her too-tight white uniform were open, exposing an eye-catching cleavage. She was slowly chewing gum and smiling at Rivera.

"You Beefcakes want some breakfast?" she asked in a sultry voice.

"I'll have pancakes and a slice of ham," said Mitchell.

"I'll have my usual," said Rivera.

"Eggs over easy, sausage, hash browns, and wheat toast," she recited from memory. "Same thing every day." She smiled and winked at Rivera. "Maybe you should try something different once in a while. Know what I mean?"

She jotted the orders into her pad and left just as quickly as she'd appeared.

Rivera hoped he wasn't blushing.

Mitchell laughed. "She's still got a thing for you, doesn't she?"

"It's all harmless. She's a good friend. She's been bringing me breakfast since the day I arrived in Moab."

Mitchell sipped his coffee. "I heard you had a wolf sighting in the LaSals. Everyone in my county is talking about it. If wolves get established in the LaSals, the Abajos will be next. When that happens, there's bound to be trouble in my county."

"Yeah. They've been declared an endangered species, so it's against the law to kill them. So we'll just have to find a way to coexist."

"Right, but what's a cattleman supposed to do if wolves are raiding his herd and killing his calves? This is going to be a problem for all of us."

Rivera nodded. "I know. And sooner or later, we'll be caught in the middle of it."

Betty returned with their breakfast, slid their plates in front of them, and left.

Halfway through breakfast, Rivera looked around to make sure no one was within earshot, then leaned forward and lowered his voice. "Do you remember that girl who drove off Hwy 128 and plunged to her death? The one who had been experimenting with peyote?"

Mitchell raised his eyebrows. He leaned forward and spoke in a whisper. "The Navarro girl? Yeah, sure. What about her?"

"This is for your ears only." Rivera knew he could trust Mitchell. They'd been sharing law enforcement secrets since Rivera was a rookie deputy. "The DEA ordered us to stay out of it. They say the Navarro incident may be tied to a larger peyote investigation they're conducting. Not only do they want us to stay out of it, they also want us to keep silent about their involvement in the case."

"That's not unusual. The feds are always sticking their noses into our business. You remember that ancient-Indian pottery business in 2009 when the FBI descended on Blanding like a bunch of locusts? They were wearing SWAT gear and arrested a bunch of our finest citizens for having pottery collections. They'd never seriously enforced the laws protecting ancient-Indian artifacts before, so collectors had operated with impunity for decades. Most of the locals grew up believing that digging them up was okay. Then the feds decided to start enforcing the law. They wanted to start with some high-profile arrests that would make the national news. Teach everyone a lesson. So they came to town and tore a hole in the community's heart. They didn't tell Sheriff Zilic a damn thing about what they were planning to do. They surprised all of us. Then they made us assist after-the-fact which sure didn't engender the affection of our citizens toward us deputies."

"I remember hearing about that. It happened before I came to Moab. The problem in the Navarro case is the father. We're not permitted to tell him that the DEA is investigating the matter, and we're not permitted to get involved in the investigation ourselves, so he thinks no one in law enforcement is looking into his daughter's death. He must think we don't care about him or his daughter. It's frustrating. Have you had any peyote cases in San Juan County in recent years?"

Mitchell thought for a long moment. "We had one about three years ago. Wasn't much of a thing. A Navajo who belonged to the Native American Church—and could therefore obtain and use peyote legally in the church's religious ceremonies—was selling it on the street in Bluff. I believe he's still in prison. Other than that, I don't think we've had much trouble with peyote."

Rivera wasn't aware of the peyote exemption for members of the Native American Church. "So how does that work? How does peyote get distributed only to Native American Church members?"

"Honestly Manny, I don't know much about it. You'll have to ask someone who's better informed on the subject."

"Okay. If you hear anything more about illegal peyote use in San Juan County, let me know about it. I'm very interested."

"Will do." Mitchell looked at his watch. "Manny, I've got to run. Sheriff Zilic called an early morning meeting of all deputies. Nothing serious going on. He just likes to give us all a pep talk from time to time and tell us how important we are to the community." He finished his coffee, placed some cash on the table, and left the diner.

Rivera looked out the window. The edge of the sun was barely visible over the peaks now. It looked like it was going to be another beautiful day in Moab. He was glad he'd discovered Moab. It all started when his high school class took a chartered bus trip from Las Cruces to Moab to visit Arches National Park. He was instantly and forever hooked on the area when he saw the unforgettable red rock formations everywhere he looked. He vowed someday to return. After college and the law enforcement academy, he served as a city cop in Las Cruces for four years, all the while looking for an opportunity to move to Moab. Finally he was offered a job as a deputy sheriff working under Sheriff Leroy Bradshaw. He'd decided he wanted to spend the rest of his life living here. Then Gloria came into his world. For him, it was a storybook tale. Now, if they were blessed with a family, his life would be complete. He smiled as he imagined playing ball with a son and reading children's books to a daughter.

Then the thought that he and Gloria might never have kids occurred to him. That made his heart sink and produced in him a feeling of emptiness. He pushed the thought out of his mind just as Betty arrived back at the table. She leaned forward and refilled Rivera's coffee mug. She lingered there, looking at him with a smile on her face. Rivera didn't know whether to avert his eyes or not. Finally, she stood up straight, as if a new thought had occurred to her.

"I'll bet I know something you don't know," she said.

"What's that?"

"Oh, it's something you'd definitely like to know."

"What is it?"

"I'm not sure I'm going to reveal it just yet."

"Are you going to tell me or just tease me?"

She leaned forward and wiped some toast crumbs off the table. "Mmm. I love the thought of teasing you. You look so yummy in that uniform."

"C'mon Betty. What is it?"

"Beg me."

Rivera laughed and played along. "Please?"

"All right. Your boss has a boyfriend."

"Ah. I suspected as much. Do you know who he is?"

"Yes, I do."

"Are you going to tell me?"

"Not yet."

"Why not?"

"Beg me."

"C'mon Betty. Tell me."

"Oh, all right. It's the sheriff of Mesa County in Colorado. His name is Bob Henderson. They met at a law enforcement conference."

"That's great. I'm happy to hear it. How did you find out?"

She looked at him with a wry expression and slowly shook her head. "As I've told you many times before, the Rim Rock Diner is like a black hole for information. Sooner or later, all juicy rumors and gossip make their way to the ears of the waitresses in our humble café. Of course, we're obligated to never repeat what we hear, like priests in a confessional. But I've made an exception in your case, so you owe me."

"Well, thanks for letting me know."

"There's just one problem, though. I'm having a hard time dealing with the thought of two sheriffs smooching."

Rivera laughed. "I've got to run."

8

RIVERA WAS STILL GRINNING as he walked out of the diner. He climbed into his vehicle, pulled his cell phone from his pocket, and called Chris Carey. He hoped to learn more from his journalist friend about peyote and the Native American Church. Rivera had mixed feelings about narcotics, and his feelings were not always consistent with the letter of the law. It had always been his philosophy to handle teenagers experimenting with drugs not as criminals, but rather as kids who made a mistake as they learned about life. His reaction was always to visit the parents, inform them that their kid was using, and request that they handle it. With pushers, it was a different matter. It was in their best financial interest to get a kid hooked and then gradually motivate him to try stronger and potentially more lethal drugs. With pushers, Rivera would do everything in his power to arrest them and lock them up for a long time.

He was vaguely familiar with peyote and its effects. Like marijuana and cocaine, it was a plant-based narcotic which has been in use by indigenous peoples in the Americas throughout recorded history, but one rarely read about it in the newspapers. Rivera waited and listened to the phone buzz six times before Carey answered it.

"Hello?" Carey sounded out of breath.

"Chris, it's Manny. Did I catch you at a bad time?"

"No problem, Manny. I just got in from this morning's walk. Three miles. My doc says I've got to get cardio exercise daily to stay healthy, especially considering my advanced years. Later today, I'll go to my little weight room and pump some iron."

Rivera was immediately reminded that he hadn't been keeping up with his resolution to get more exercise. "That's what I should be doing. Gloria smiled and patted me on the stomach the other day. I think she was sending me a message."

"It's a lot easier to find time to exercise when you don't have a job. What can I help you with this morning?"

"Chris, I'm interested in peyote. Are you up to speed on the Native American Church and the legal exemption they have for using a controlled substance in their religious ceremonies? I've heard a little about it, but I need to understand the larger picture."

"I assume this has to do with the Navarro girl who was killed in that auto accident a while back."

"Yes, and this discussion must be off the record. The DEA has ordered us to stay out of the peyote business."

"Of course. As far as I'm concerned, all our discussions involving your cases are off the record."

"I appreciate that. Thanks."

"I did a lot of research on peyote years ago for a piece I was writing when I worked for The Salt Lake City Tribune. It's an interesting mixture of religion, geography, and laws. Peyote is a small, squatty-looking barrel cactus that grows in northern Mexico and in four Texas counties along the Rio Grande River. Have you ever seen it?"

"I've seen pictures of it, but that's all."

"There's not much to it. It's a spineless cactus that grows close to the ground. It has kind of a light grayish-green color that blends into the terrain, so it's hard to spot. You could walk past one and not even notice it. When it blooms in the springtime, it produces tiny pinkish-white flowers. It contains mescaline, a hallucinogenic chemical that will put you on a psychedelic trip. So, that's the plant. As far as its use is concerned, Native American tribes have been using it for millennia for medicinal and ceremonial purposes. The Native American Church came along in the late-1800s and used it in their religious rites and rituals. As they explain it, their goal of using peyote is not to get high, but to connect better with the creator and promote healing and fellowship. They consider it sacramental."

"But some people are using it these days simply to get high."

"True. But that's not the intention of the church. Anyway, peyote use was illegal in the U.S. for a long time, but based on freedom of religion arguments, the Supreme Court decided that its use in Native American Church religious ceremonies was legal. But to ensure that its distribution was limited to the church, the law was changed to permit *peyoteros*—people who are licensed to harvest peyote—to operate in those four Texas counties. Further, the *peyoteros* are required by law to sell only to those persons who can prove they are members of the Native American Church. Now some forty tribes use it in their religious ceremonies."

"How is it harvested?"

"What the *peyoteros* do is carefully slice off the crown of the cactus—that's the part that contains the hallucinogenic buttons—and leave the base or stem in the ground so that it can regrow. The buttons are then sold to church members. Some refer to them as sacred buttons. In some cases, the entire cactus is harvested and sold."

Rivera considered that. "There must be lots of ways peyote gets into the hands of the general public."

"Sure. Every time the government outlaws something, they create a black market in the process. A lot of it is smuggled in from Mexico—both plants and seeds. Some of it comes illegally from Texas too. In recent years, you can buy the stuff online and pay for it with a cryptocurrency to keep the transaction shielded from the eyes of the law."

Rivera shook his head. "Sounds like an impossible law enforcement situation. Okay, thanks for the help, Chris."

9

RIVERA PARKED AT the curb in front of a two-story gray brick house that corresponded to the address on Derek Webster's driver's license. It was on a tree-lined street in a quiet neighborhood, away from the tourist hustle and bustle on Main Street. Rose bushes grew around the perimeter of the front yard, and a graceful desert willow tree stood in the center. Wooden steps led up to a covered porch with two rocking chairs. Colorful blocks of agate and petrified wood lined the front edge of the porch. A woman who appeared to be in her late fifties was trimming the rose bushes along the edge of the driveway. She looked up as Rivera stepped out of his vehicle.

"You're here about Derek's death, aren't you?" Her expression was troubled.

"Yes, Ma'am."

"I'm Lisa Bennett. My husband and I live here. We rented Derek the cabana behind our house. My Uncle Pete lived there before he died. He had to use a wheelchair for mobility because of a war injury he sustained in Viet Nam. So the cabana was already equipped with ramps and grab bars. It seemed ideal for Derek. We park in front of the house so Derek can use the driveway all the way back to the cabana."

"I'd like to ask you a few questions about him."

"Of course. Let's go sit inside. Terrible thing what happened to that poor man."

They entered the house, and she led him into a living room furnished with a traditional overstuffed couch and matching chairs. The tables and shelves were filled with framed family photographs, dozens of colorful rock samples, and three Hopi kachinas. Rivera's nostrils detected a pleasant fragrance that he couldn't identify. They sat in chairs facing one other. A tabby cat sleeping on the couch opened its eyes, looked at the intruder, stretched its legs, and yawned. It rolled over on its side and went back to sleep.

Rivera extracted a pen and notepad from his shirt pocket. "How long have you been renting to Derek?"

"Almost two years."

"Do you know where he lived before he moved into the cabana?"

"Yes, he lived in a cabin at his father's place. His father owns that nursery near Dewey Bridge."

"Do you know what motivated him to move?"

"He said he wanted to start a new life. Before the accident where he lost the use of his feet, he was an avid backcountry hiker. When fate took his favorite activity away from him, he moved into the cabin on his father's property. There was little he could do to help with the nursery operation, so he kind of felt useless. He said he was beginning to feel like a dependent and that made him even more despondent. After a life of backcountry exploring, you can certainly understand that. Anyway, that's when he began drinking a lot. Then one day he became acquainted with drones. He imagined he could use drones as a kind of substitute for hiking, and that helped him get off the booze. Soon after that, he was practicing what he called virtual hiking nearly every day. His father wanted him to stay at the cabin, but Derek wanted a normal life surrounded by people and activities. His father finally understood and reluctantly helped him find a new place and move his belongings. Lucky for us, Derek came here."

"What kind of person was he?"

"He was wonderful. A thoughtful gentleman. Despite his handicap, he led as normal a life as he could. He didn't own a wheelchair. He had a pair of crutches back in the cabana, but I'd rarely seen him use them. I think he was bound and determined to get along without them. It was a pride thing, I believe. I never heard him complain about his limited mobility or anything else for that matter. He was interesting and upbeat. Always paid his rent on time. I couldn't have asked for a better tenant. I feel such a loss. My husband Fred is a rockhound, so he and Derek spent a lot of time together talking about rocks and geology, and whether drones could be used to locate interesting rock samples. They were trying to figure out a way to go rockhounding together." She chuckled. "They were also planning some Halloween stunts using one of Derek's drones. You know, hanging a flowing white sheet with a scary face from the drone, zooming in above the kids, and scaring them with a ghostly voice from a speaker. Derek could be mischievous and fun. Fred said he and Derek were also talking about forming a club for kids interested in drones and robots. My husband and I had grown very fond of him. We often had him over for dinner. He was like family. That's why I was outside trimming rose bushes that didn't really need to be trimmed. It helps me deal with what happened."

"Aside from you and your husband, did he have friends, people he saw on a regular basis?"

"Well, there was his girlfriend, Evelyn Ellwood. They met back in February. I saw Evelyn here a lot. We got to be friends."

"Where does she live?"

"In Moab." She gave Rivera the address and phone number. "As soon as I heard the news last night about Derek, I rushed over to her place to tell her, or just be with her if she'd already heard. She'd already heard. Guy Richardson, who works for Derek's father, called her late yesterday afternoon and broke the news. She was in tears the whole time I was there. The poor thing. She's such a sweet girl. I had the impression she and Derek were thinking about getting married, but I'm not sure."

"Any other friends you know about?"

"He had visitors, mostly men. Only one stands out. He was an older, bald guy who I saw visiting Derek several times. He was overweight and always seemed to be chomping on a cigar. I don't think they were close friends, at least that's my impression. Seemed more businesslike. The other visitors came and went. Some more than once. I couldn't tell you much about them. Evelyn is the only one he introduced me to. Oh, and I almost forgot, his father Hal came on most Sundays and went with Derek to Denny's for breakfast. I know he must be brokenhearted."

"Do you know of any problems Derek was having?

She thought for a moment. "No, not that I'm aware of."

"Any enemies, fights, disagreements?"

"No. Everyone seemed to like Derek. He spent most of his time with Evelyn when he wasn't exploring the backcountry with his drones."

"Okay, thanks. I'm going to take a look inside his home now."

Lisa stood up. "I'll get the key and unlock the door for you."

"Thanks, but that's not necessary. I brought the keys I found in Derek's pocket. One of these should work."

"If you see Gomer back there, tell him I'll be taking care of him from now on."

"Gomer?"

"Yes. Gomer is an occasional visitor. He's a stray tomcat who saunters into the backyard every once in a while. He's all scratched up from fighting and walks with a limp. I guess Derek could relate to him. He's the one who named him and fed him whenever he showed up. Gomer is going to miss his friend."

Rivera left the house and walked up the driveway to the cabana in the rear. It was a quaint structure with its walls and peaked roof covered with wood shingles, and the door and window trim painted bright red. Potted plants in bloom lined the walkway from the driveway to the house. It looked to Rivera like something out of a fairy tale.

He pulled on a pair of latex gloves, unlocked the front door, and stepped inside. He glanced around at the interior. It was a small dwelling with a living area, bedroom, bathroom, and kitchenette. Furnishings were minimal. It struck Rivera as odd that, except for a television, there was a total absence of electronic gear in the home. No drones, no computers, no monitors. Nothing. He expected to find at least a small lab bench with equipment to support Derek's drone operations. Rivera wondered if maybe everything Derek needed was in his Bronco Raptor.

The kitchenette was equipped with the standard appliances: a toaster, can opener, coffee maker, microwave, stove, and refrigerator. He opened the refrigerator door and inspected the contents. Milk, meat, butter, eggs, and an assortment of fruits and vegetables. In the sink were dishes and utensils soaking in soapy water. An unopened bottle of inexpensive red wine sat on the countertop.

The bathroom was small and fitted with grab bars and ramps to make it handicapped accessible. The medicine cabinet contained a bottle of aspirin, a tube of toothpaste, two toothbrushes, floss, a razor, shaving cream, and after-shave. Nothing unusual caught his eye.

The bedroom was furnished with a queen-size bed, a dresser, and a bedside table with a single drawer. A hiking guide to Cedar Mesa rested on top of the table. In the drawer he found two more hiking books and a Glock nine-millimeter handgun. He picked up the gun, released the magazine, pulled back the slide, and caught the ejected bullet. He sniffed the chamber—the gun had not recently been fired. He placed the gun, magazine, and bullet into evidence bags. Later he would run the gun's serial number through the FBI's firearms database to see if it had a history on record, but he didn't expect to learn anything incriminating—many good citizens owned handguns for personal protection.

He checked the small closet adjacent to the bedroom and saw clothing on hangers and several pairs of shoes on the floor. The shoes looked specially made to fit prosthetic feet.

He returned to the living room which was furnished with two overstuffed chairs and a small couch positioned in front of the television. Against the wall was a tall bookcase containing dozens of hiking guidebooks, novels by Zane Grey and other Southwest authors, and map atlases for Utah, Colorado, New Mexico, and Arizona. He glanced at the titles of some of the hiking guidebooks. They were well used and pretty much covered the most interesting parts of the Four Corners area. Many were authored by Michael Kelsey, a man serious hikers considered a guru and whose hiking routes were generally not for the faint of heart.

There were also two framed photographs on the shelves, one of Derek and a grinning lady with mussed hair wearing jeans and a sweatshirt, the other of the same lady in a more formal pose wearing a flowery blue blouse.

Spread out on the coffee table was a half-inch stack of U.S.G.S topographic maps. Rivera paged through them and saw that they covered most of southeast Utah and a narrow slice of western Colorado. The map on top of the pile included Warner Lake and the surrounding area. The place from which Derek had launched the drone yesterday was circled in pencil. Other places on that map and other maps had circles drawn on them as well. Were these all launching points for Derek's drone flights in the past? Rivera figured they were. He sat back and thought about the maps. It wasn't unusual for a lover of canyons, mesas, and mountains to have a strong interest in maps.

Derek's home was minimal, just a place to eat and sleep. There were few decorative items, and the walls were bare, except for a framed print of Landscape Arch.

Rivera turned on the television, saw that it was tuned to a stock market channel, and shut it off.

He locked the door, strung crime scene tape around the house, and returned to his pickup. His impression of Derek Webster thus far was that he was a solid citizen who fell on hard times, but through diligence and perseverance was able to get his life back on track. He wished he had known the man. He seemed like the kind of person Rivera would choose for a friend.

He drove to Evelyn Ellwood's house a few blocks away, parked at the curb, and rang her doorbell.

10

WHEN THE DOOR opened, Rivera saw a distraught woman wearing a white terrycloth bathrobe. She looked exhausted. Her large brown eyes were bloodshot, and her blonde hair was disheveled. She was thin and pretty, maybe in her late twenties. She matched the framed photos of the girl in Derek's cabana. He introduced himself and apologized for the intrusion. She nodded and gestured for him to come inside and take a seat. She had a shy, introverted manner and seemed preoccupied with her thoughts.

Rivera regretted bothering her at a time like this, but his investigation couldn't wait. "I'm very sorry for your loss. I'm investigating Derek's death and wanted to learn as much as I can about him and his activities."

Her eyes widened. "Are you saying someone killed him on purpose?"

"We don't know. Any shooting death requires an investigation and it's a possibility we have to consider."

"That can't possibly be. Everyone loved Derek."

"How long have you known him?"

"We met about eight months ago." She sighed with a forlorn look.

"How did you meet?"

"I was waiting tables at La Jacaranda Mexican Restaurant, and he came in by himself. It was the middle of the afternoon, and the place was kind of empty. We got to talking and instantly hit it off. We started seeing each other a lot after that. For the last few weeks, we've even been talking about getting married." Her lower lip protruded and began quivering. "I loved him so much. This was the first time in my life I felt that way and look what happened. I'm so unlucky. I've always been unlucky." She put her hands to her face and burst into tears.

Rivera waited a long moment until she composed herself. "Can you tell me how he spent most of his time—I mean when he wasn't with you?"

"He loved the backcountry. He talked about it like it was a real person. Almost a best friend. He often went exploring by himself. At first, I was real worried about his safety, considering his prostheses—but he always came back."

"What did he do when he wasn't away in the backcountry?"

"He spent a lot of time with me. We'd usually have dinner together. I'm a pretty good cook so most of the time we ate at my place. Sometimes I help in the kitchen at La Jacaranda, so I know how to make really good enchiladas, which Derek loved. Once in a while, he'd help me cook. Other times we'd go out for dinner at one of the local restaurants. Our evenings were simple. We just liked being together. We'd watch movies on television or play cards or a board game with Lisa and Fred Bennett. They own the cabana that Derek rents. Sometimes we'd go out to the movies." She continued to ramble on about things they'd done together, seemingly lost in her thoughts.

Rivera patiently listened. "Did he ever go into the backcountry with other people?"

"Occasionally he took me with him. Other times, he went with people who paid him to help them explore. That was his new business. He started it a couple of months ago, and it was beginning to work out well for him. He didn't need the money—he had plenty after the accident settlement—but he just enjoyed doing it. He never said so, but I think it made him feel more like a normal person with a job and some regular income. It was as though he really wasn't handicapped."

"Do you know much about the business end of his activities? Who hired him, what types of services he provided, and so forth?"

She shook her head. "Not much. I know he helped hunters and some private investigator he knew."

That got Rivera's attention. "Do you know the name of the private investigator?"

"No. I never met him." Her lip began quivering again. "I can't believe he's gone. I thought my life was finally on track. I met a good man and wanted to spend the rest of my life with him." She shook her head. "I'm a high school dropout and I had no prospects until I met Derek. He gave me a chance at a normal life. What am I going to do now?" Her sobs were uncontrollable.

Rivera knew he had overstayed his welcome. He stood up. "I'm sorry for your loss. We can talk again another time. Is there a friend you can call?" When she nodded, he let himself out and closed the door. He could fill in any additional details he needed later, after the poor woman had time to deal with Derek's death. Rivera felt like a heel for intruding.

He thought about Derek, a man like hundreds of other backcountry adventurers who loved exploring the high desert and enjoyed its remoteness and its beauty. That is, until he had his accident. Then everything changed for him. His new circumstances caused him to innovate and find a way to hike the canyons and mesas without going on foot. Using a drone would certainly make him a unique figure in the hiking community. Was it this difference that made him stand out as a target for some deranged psycho? And what was Derek doing for a private investigator? Had he stuck his nose into some business that had gotten him killed?

11

RIVERA'S NEXT STOP was the home of Charlie Savage, a technical guru and friend who often helped the deputy in matters involving technology. Rivera was grateful to have someone with Savage's expertise to consult with and learn from. Technology was not one of the deputy's strengths, and Savage was generous with his time and seemed to enjoy helping out.

Rivera parked in front of Savage's house and walked to the detached garage Savage had converted years ago into a first-class laboratory. He spent most of his time there working on technical projects that interested him. He was much more likely to be in his laboratory than his house.

Rivera peered through the small window in the side door and saw Savage sitting on a stool at one of the lab benches. He was wearing a baggy white shirt, khaki shorts, and sandals. His brown hair was shoulder length and he looked just as overweight as the last time Rivera had seen him, despite his stated desire to lose a few pounds. The place hadn't changed much. There were a half-dozen lab benches filled with expensive electronic equipment and a machine shop in the rear.

When Rivera tapped on the glass, Savage looked up, smiled, and waved him in. "Hi Manny. What's going on?"

Rivera was always impressed by the cleanliness and brightness of Savage's laboratory. The walls, ceiling, and floor were all painted white, giving the lab a kind of glowing, almost antiseptic appearance. Savage was sitting in front of a large circuit board and some loose electronic components. He was holding a smoldering soldering iron in one hand and a spool of solder in the other.

"Charlie, I need some help."

"Sure, Manny. What can I do for you?" He returned the soldering iron to its stand and placed the solder on the bench.

"Did you hear about the shooting death in the mountains yesterday?"

Savage's eyebrows went up. "No, I didn't. Who got shot?"

"A man named Derek Webster from Moab. Did you know him?"

Savage's face froze. He was silent for a long moment. "Yes, I did know him. What happened?"

"He was shot in the back while using a drone to help a couple of bow hunters locate a bull elk. How well did you know him?"

Savage reached out and retrieved a cupcake from an open package on the bench, stuffed the whole thing into his mouth, and slowly chewed it. He washed it down with a swig of cola and shook his head. "Personally, not very well. But a couple of years ago I helped him get started with drones. I set up all his drone equipment and showed him how to use it. Was the shooting an accident?"

"Just between the two of us Charlie, I don't think so." Rivera explained his reasoning. "Dead center shot into a bright orange vest with two vehicles parked nearby."

"Yeah, I see what you mean. But why would anyone want to shoot Derek? He was a really good guy. Clean cut and friendly."

"That's what I aim to find out."

"I'll be glad to help you any way I can."

Rivera was eager to learn all he could about drones and how they worked, but first he wanted to understand how Derek got started in the drone business. "How did you first meet him?"

"He contacted me out of the blue one day. He said he'd heard about my electronics capabilities from someone in town and wanted to explore an idea with me. He told me about losing his feet in an auto accident and that he was no longer able to do the things he loved, namely hiking and exploring the backcountry. He couldn't hike very far, and he certainly couldn't navigate a rough trail, so he wanted to use a drone to simulate hiking. His goal was to be able to drive into the mountains, launch a drone, and guide it down a canyon, all the while looking at the video image from an onboard camera. So I designed a system that would meet his needs and gave him a list of what to buy. When the equipment was delivered, I taught him how to hook it up and operate it. I went with him on his first couple of forays to make sure everything worked okay and that he knew how to operate it. He was a quick study and caught on fast. That's how it all started."

"I just came from his house. I was surprised to find there was no electronic equipment there. I thought he'd have a lab setup somewhere. You know, to support the equipment he had in his vehicle."

"He does. He rented a storage unit at EZ'S Self Storage on South Main. It's arranged like a small lab with an office. At first, he had set it up on tables in that little cabana he rented."

"Why did he move it?"

"He needed more space, but he also said it was for security reasons. He had a lot of money invested in the equipment and wanted to make sure no one pilfered it. He said his little house was too easy to break into. As the months went by, he bought more and more gear. I think he owned a half dozen drones and some sophisticated video cameras, including a couple of infrared jobs. He was an intelligent guy and became proficient in operating the equipment faster than I had expected. I haven't heard from him in a long time, so I assumed everything was operating okay."

"You know how ignorant I am about electronics. How about going to the storage unit with me and explaining what he's got in there?"

"Sure, Manny. Have you got a key?"

"I've got his keyring with me. I'm guessing one of the keys will fit the lock."

They rode in Rivera's vehicle to EZ'S Self Storage, Savage guiding the deputy to Derek's unit.

Rivera selected what appeared to be the correct key, inserted it into the heavy-duty lock on the roll-up door, and twisted it. The lock popped open. He removed it and raised the door. They stepped inside and Savage reached for a wall switch and turned on the lights. Rivera was amazed by what he saw. The storage unit was ten feet wide and twelve feet deep. It contained a gray metal desk, two chairs, a small refrigerator, a case of bottled water, and a lab bench filled with an impressive array of electronic equipment. A computer sat on the desk, along with a coffee maker and a mug. A shelf of technical manuals was attached to the wall behind the desk. Hanging on the far wall were a half dozen drones of different sizes and propellor configurations.

Savage sat down in front of the computer and turned it on. A color monitor came to life with a screen saver. "I'll bet Derek never changed the password I used when I first set up the system. I remember it was the name of a dog we had when I was a youngster. We kids called him

Elephant Face. Elfie for short." He typed in *elephantface* and smiled when the system accepted it.

"Elephant Face?" asked Rivera.

"He was a funny looking dog. A mutt with flappy ears and a long nose that we kids thought looked like a trunk."

Savage showed Rivera how to access the list of files stored in the computer. "Each file has a unique name with a date. The date corresponds to when the file was first established. Let's pick one at random from the list and see what's in it." He clicked on a file entitled Hideout Canyon 6-8-22, then clicked on the *Start* icon.

"Take a look, Manny. It's a video recording of what the drone's camera saw as it passed through the canyon. The *Plus* and *Minus* icons allow you to zoom in and out of the image on the screen."

The image was in high-fidelity color. They watched as the drone moved steadily ahead through the canyon for several minutes, the cottonwood trees and junipers passing by below. Soon the drone came upon a narrow side canyon and stopped. It moved slowly toward the side canyon, as if inspecting it. The red rock walls were streaked with desert varnish and patches of the canyon floor were purple with sagebrush in bloom. Shafts of sunlight created dappled shadows throughout the scene. The drone stopped again, looked left, then right, then moved ahead slowly until it came upon a small panel of petroglyphs which included spirals, several shaman figures, a long snake, a four-legged animal with horns, a long row of dots, and a Kokopelli image. The drone then continued farther up the side canyon. Savage clicked on the *Pause* icon and the video stopped.

"See, Manny, that's all there is to it. Turn on the monitor, click on the file you want to see, and start the video."

"You know, I think Derek was right. Watching that video gives one a similar feeling to actually hiking through the canyon. There's a lot missing, of course. The sense of being alone in the wilderness, listening to the birds singing in the trees, inhaling the fresh air, feeling your heart pump as you hike up a hill, and so forth. But clearly, it's way better than sitting home watching television."

"Think you can do it now?"

"I think so. I'll give it a try." Rivera chose another file, clicked *Start*, and watched as the drone moved slowly down the Colorado River. On the way, it explored a couple of side canyons, lingered over an armada of colorful rafts with waving occupants, and reached the U.S. 191 bridge where it turned south into Moab. It flew up Main Street and eventually landed in Rotary Park. Rivera smiled, enjoying the experience. "I think I've got it, Charlie."

"Try another one, just to be sure."

Rivera selected another file and repeated the process. This time, he had the sensation of flying across a mesa top close to the ground, following the undulations of the rolling topography. Below him passed a seemingly infinite expanse of sagebrush interspersed with dark green junipers. A flock of bluebirds scattered as the drone passed over them. The drone then crossed over a large canyon and continued flying over the table land on the other side. To Rivera, it was a thoroughly enjoyable experience—almost like an amusement park ride. He had the urge to stay and view a few more files but felt compelled to get on with his investigation.

"Manny, if you want to move one of these files to your office computer, you can transmit it as an attachment to an email or write it to one of those thumb drives and carry it to your office." He pointed to an open package of thumb drives.

"Thanks, Charlie. I don't want to take too much of your time, but I wonder if you have time to go with me to the Sheriff's impound lot and give me a quick tutorial on how to operate the equipment mounted in Derek's vehicle."

"Sure, Manny. Glad to."

12

RIVERA DROVE SAVAGE to the impound lot, unlocked the gate, and parked next to Derek Webster's Ford Bronco Raptor. He unlocked the Raptor and swung open the rear door to give Savage access to the equipment.

"It looks pretty much the same as the last time I saw it," said Savage. "Derek and I positioned these two racks in the rear of the Raptor so he could sit in a chair behind the vehicle and be at eye-level with the equipment. We bolted the racks securely to the floor and then mounted the electronic instruments onto the racks."

"Can you show me how it all works?"

"Sure. The first thing you need to know is how the instruments are powered. There's an inverter mounted in the right rack that converts the vehicle's 12-volt battery power to 120-volt A.C. power. That's distributed to each of the instruments. You don't want the battery to go dead because of the continuous power drain, so it's best to keep the engine idling while you're using the system. Let's start the engine and I'll show you how everything works."

Rivera started the engine and let it idle.

Savage turned on the master switch and the system came to life. Red "power-on" lights on each instrument glowed, and the monitors came to life.

"Okay. The monitor on the right shows whatever the camera on the drone is looking at. The monitor on the left shows a topo map of the area and the red dot indicates the location of the drone. The drone knows its location because it has a GPS receiver on board.

"Just below the monitor on the right are the controls for the drone. You can fly the drone in any direction or rotate it or tip it or change its altitude. You can also pan the camera up and down." Savage pointed to the controls as he spoke. There were two joysticks and an array of knobs, switches, and lights.

He pointed out to Rivera the transmitter which allowed control signals to be sent to the drone and the receiver which captured the video signals from the drone's onboard camera. He pointed out the indicator that displayed how much power remained in the drone's battery, and the master control computer which stored the incoming video images. There was also a recharge station for the drone's battery pack at the bottom of the left rack. Lastly, he talked about battery life, flight time, and the range of the system. "In the absence of wind, this type of drone will operate for about an hour and a half."

Rivera felt bombarded with information but understood the basics of the system.

Savage opened the side door of the vehicle exposing a spare drone. He said Derek always brought along a backup drone in case of a mishap. He pointed out the different subsystems mounted on the drone: the transmit and receive modules, the GPS unit, the camera, and the four propellors, and explained how each worked.

"You have to be careful when you fly one of these into a canyon. You might lose your transmit/receive connection and never be able to bring the drone back. We learned that the hard way. So I added some software that detected a loss of signal and automatically commanded the unit to fly straight up until connectivity was restored."

Rivera was impressed. "That's very clever."

Savage smiled. "Do you want me to launch the drone so you can fly it around for a while? See how it feels?"

Rivera considered that for a moment. It would be fun to pilot a drone up and down Moab's streets for a few minutes. Fun but not necessary. Furthermore, he didn't want to fly it into a wall and damage evidence or get it hung up in a tree. "No, thanks. For now, I just need to know how it operates."

"Maybe another time. I'm always available."

"Can I get a replay of what the drone saw on its flight yesterday?"

"Sure. It should be stored in the computer's memory. Savage moved the mouse and clicked on a couple of icons while Rivera peered over his shoulder. Soon, the monitor on the right showed a freeze frame displaying some trees and the blurred face of a man who looked like Derek. "If you want to view the whole video, just click on the *Play* icon and it should show you the entire flight from yesterday."

"Okay, thanks, Charlie. I don't want to take up any more of your time than necessary. I don't know how long that video is, but I can watch it after I take you home."

"That's fine by me, Manny. I don't really want to watch a prelude to the death of a guy I knew. I tend to have nightmares. I'm afraid I'll see something I can't unsee."

Rivera drove back to Savage's place and dropped him off. The deputy thanked him profusely for all his help.

"Glad to help, Manny. Call me if you have any more questions."

Rivera was eager to view the video. He returned to the impound lot, started the Raptor's engine, and opened the rear door. He initiated the video stored in the computer. He was surprised at how much less intimidating the equipment looked compared to the first time he'd seen it, now that he had the benefit of Savage's tutelage. His favorite instructor in college once told him, "Everything's easy, once you know how." How true.

He started the video file stored in the system's computer and watched the monitor. At first it showed some erratic and blurry patterns of scenery, then it stabilized showing trees and sky. The drone circled twice above the area where the Raptor was parked. On the third pass, Derek must have panned the camera downward because Rivera could now see the two bow hunters, the Raptor, and Derek himself. The drone rocked back and forth for a few moments, then sped off above the road Rivera had used to access the crime scene. It skirted over Warner Lake and returned to its starting point. Rivera figured Derek had been checking the controls before sending the drone on its mission, wanting to ensure that everything was in proper working order.

From there, the drone headed east and dipped into a shallow canyon. Rivera watched intently, looking for any clue that might be related to Derek's death. Trees and rock formations whizzed by as the drone flew up the canyon. Rivera judged its speed at about fifteen miles per hour. Soon the drone lifted out of the canyon and proceeded across a flat segment of open mesa. It stopped, rotated completely giving the viewer a 360-degree panoramic view, then continued on its way. Rivera imagined that here Derek was scanning the area looking for any sign of an elk herd. The drone paused over what appeared to be a hunter, most likely a male judging by his size, who had a rifle strapped to his back and was supporting himself with a walking stick. He was wearing a wide-brimmed hat with what looked like a large feather protruding from the hat band. Farther down the canyon about two miles, the drone passed over a second hunter who was sitting on the ground, apparently resting. He wore an orange hat and had a rifle resting across his lap.

A few minutes later, the drone spotted a trio of men about a hundred yards up a side canyon. The drone paused and the camera watched for a brief moment. They appeared to be digging in the dirt in front of a south-facing, red-rock alcove. Rivera surmised they were excavating an ancient-Indian midden pile in search of artifacts. Either they were serious anthropologists with a permit in search of new knowledge on how the old ones lived, or they were thieves ransacking a site in the hope of finding valuable artifacts they could sell. Rivera recorded the GPS coordinates of the site in his notepad.

The drone exited the canyon and flew over a mesa top for several minutes before arriving at a second canyon, this one larger, and descended into its depths. There were red rock walls on both sides and the floor was populated with sagebrush, pinyon pines, and cottonwoods. The drone recorded another hunter or perhaps a hiker who was barely visible through the trees, then continued down the canyon. Twenty minutes later, the canyon ended, and wide-open mesa land was reached. The drone stopped as a small herd of elk came into view. There were nine of them grazing in an open field populated with scattered junipers, and a prize bull was in their midst.

The drone then veered off and backed away from the herd. It remained motionless for a long period, just watching the animals. This must have been when Derek gave instructions to the bow hunters on how to navigate toward the herd's location, and they set out on their journey. Ten minutes later, the drone plummeted to the ground and the video abruptly ended. Rivera figured this was the moment when Derek was shot. He must have fallen forward against the joystick controls, sending the drone to its demise. Rivera saw no obvious reason to suspect that anyone who appeared in the video was the shooter, but he would sure like to find them and ask them a few questions. Identifying them, he realized, would likely be impossible.

Rivera looked at the red dot on the small monitor. The drone was about three miles from the place where Derek had been shot. Three miles of tough hiking. And according to the time stamp on the video, he was killed at 1:06 pm.

Rivera powered down the equipment, shut off the Raptor's engine, and locked the vehicle. He climbed into his pickup and sat there thinking. He'd learned a little more about Derek Webster and how he went about making a profit from his drone business, but nothing that suggested a motive for his murder. He decided to return to Derek's storage unit and take a closer look at the information stored in the computer there. Maybe he could find a lead somewhere in those files.

13

RIVERA UNLOCKED THE storage unit and turned on the lights. He closed the door behind him for privacy and glanced at his surroundings, impressed by the level of technology Derek was able to acquire and master. The drones hanging on the wall came in several sizes and were equipped with different types of cameras and propellor configurations. Rivera was feeling more comfortable with the technology that surrounded him. It no longer looked totally foreign. He sat down at the desk, glancing around the room and wondering where to start.

His eyes fell upon the row of books on the shelf behind the desk. Two heavy chunks of multicolored agate served as bookends. All of the books looked like technical manuals with printed titles and corporate names on the spines, except for one. The exception was a smaller, thinner black book that appeared to be a notebook or journal of some kind. Rivera pulled it out and opened it.

On the first page were written the words *Webster Drone Services,* and below that *Open for Business.* There, Derek had drawn a happy face. The entry was dated eight weeks ago. Rivera thumbed through the contents of the journal. Each page contained handwritten notes which seemed to describe paying projects for which Derek had been hired.

The first project was dated seven weeks ago and contained information regarding an assignment that Rivera figured was Derek's first paying job:

> *Client: Phil Broderick*
>
> *Fee: $600 per day*
>
> *Computer File: Broderick001*
>
> *From Moab*
>
> *Wife: Ginny Hempstead*
>
> *Husband: Gene Squires*
>
> *Husband meets Blonde each Monday and Thursday at 4:00 p.m. at Miner's Basin Trailhead, between 4 and 5 pm. Wife needs documented proof of husband's infidelity.*

Rivera couldn't help but smile. Phil Broderick must be the private investigator Evelyn Ellwood had mentioned. Derek Webster was not only in the business of helping elk hunters, he was also spying on people for a fee. Rivera shook his head. The whole business seemed totally out of place in little Moab.

Rivera turned on the computer and accessed a list of files, just the way Charlie Savage had taught him. He studied the list. It was divided into two sections, one for Derek's personal hikes and, farther down the page, a second one for Webster Drone Services. The first entry on the Webster Drone Services list was Broderick001. He clicked on the file name. The monitor came to life with images of what he guessed was the parking area at Miner's Basin trailhead. The date stamp indicated the video was recorded a little over six weeks ago. Three vehicles were parked there, and a man wearing a daypack was waiting at the trailhead. Rivera assumed he was the unfaithful Gene Squires mentioned in the notebook. Soon, a sedan drove into view and parked. A young lady with long blonde hair got out and rushed to the man's arms. They kissed and hugged passionately, then hiked on the trail until they disappeared under the forest canopy. At that point, the video ended.

He turned to the next page in the notebook. The file name was *Broderick002*. It was a repetition of the first page. So were the next four pages. He checked a calendar. The dates corresponded to Mondays and Thursdays, so Rivera assumed they would be more of the same—the drone following along as Squires and his blonde girlfriend disappeared into the woods.

The next entry in the journal was dated four weeks ago and related to elk hunting.

Client: Billy Blevins

Fee: $600 for one day

Computer file: Blevins001

Elk hunter. Wants to bag a large bull elk.

Rivera recognized the name. Blevins was the man who recommended that the Simpson brothers hire Derek to help in their search for a trophy bull elk. Rivera reviewed the video end to end. It was pretty much as he expected and very similar to the video of the Simpson brothers' hunting quest. Nothing in particular grabbed his attention.

He turned to the next page in the notebook. The entry was from three weeks ago and read:

Client: Lucas Nichols

Fee: $600 for one day

Computer file: ArtifactTheft001

Wants to know the identity of the three teenagers who are digging holes in the long-abandoned ghost town on his ranch.

Rivera turned to the computer and accessed the *ArtifactTheft001* file. After gliding across a mesa with rolling hills of sage, the video zoomed in on three people digging in the dirt in the middle of a dozen broken-down buildings constructed of wood planks. The site was not far from the Colorado River. The long-abandoned structures were small shacks which formed a tiny ghost town that looked like it dated back to the 1800s. The compound had been fenced in with barbed wire. Rivera recognized one of the individuals as Stewart Smith, the teenage son of his neighbor.

He continued paging through the journal. The next two items were repeats of the Gene Squires surveillance assignment, and the page after that was a repeat of the assignment related to the diggings at the Nichols Ranch. There were several more pages related to Phil Broderick's investigation which Rivera skipped over, figuring they were just more of the same. He turned to the following page and the word *Wolves* grabbed his attention. He read the entry which was dated five days ago:

> *Client: Rancher Group (Eddie)*
>
> *Fee: $600 per day*
>
> *Computer File: Wolves001*
>
> *Wants wolves in LaSal Mountains located and tracked. Notify Eddie immediately when I spot one. Memorize his phone number but do not write it down. A rancher saw a pair of wolves on Polar Mesa. Not far from there, he found the gutted carcass of one of his calves.*

Rivera was surprised to learn that Hazel Treadwell's wolf sighting was not the only one. A rancher had lost a calf to the wolves before Hazel called the sheriff's office. The ranchers had apparently wasted no time organizing themselves with the goal of eliminating the threat to their livelihood. And they had done so without revealing to the public what they were up to.

Rivera wondered why the rancher who had lost the calf hadn't notified the authorities. The answer came to him quickly. It would have done no good. There was nothing the law could or would do. Gray wolves were an endangered species protected by federal law. If anything was to be done about the wolves, the ranchers knew they were on their own. Rivera searched his memory for a rancher named Eddie but was unable to come up with anyone. Whoever he was, he must be anxious about security, judging by the absence of a last name and the secrecy regarding his phone number. Rivera accessed the corresponding video and clicked on *Start*.

The video showed images of typical mesa land populated with junipers, pinyon pines, and sagebrush. The drone seemed to be passing back and forth over the length of the mesa, apparently searching the entire area. Rivera watched for twenty minutes, then, his patience running out, clicked on the fast forward button. Now the image rushed by, back and forth across the mesa, until the video ended a few minutes later. It appeared Derek had not spotted a wolf on that particular day.

Rivera returned his attention to the journal. There was another Broderick entry, then the last entry referred to the Simpson brothers' search for a trophy bull elk.

Rivera called the BLM Field Office, asked for Ralph Lansing, and informed him that he had reason to believe a rancher consortium had been formed to kill wolves in the LaSals. Normally he wouldn't reveal this kind of information to anyone besides the sheriff, but he felt he owed Lansing a heads-up. He asked Lansing to keep the information confidential for the time being, at least until he had wrapped up the Derek Webster case. Lansing agreed.

That done, he closed the journal, sat back, and considered whether one of Derek's commercial activities had led to his demise. Or was it something else entirely? He had no idea, but thus far, all he had to go on were the three matters mentioned in Derek's journal: Phil Broderick's investigation of marital infidelity, the ghost town diggings, and the hunting of wolves. He would assume, at least for the time being, that Derek's murder was related to one of them. He eliminated the elk hunters as possibilities, as their activities and goals seemed straightforward. He decided to pursue the matter of the Nichols Ranch diggings first, as that seemed least likely to be the answer. He hoped to be able to eliminate it as a possibility in short order and then concentrate on the remaining two.

Rivera shut off the equipment and locked up the storage unit. The sun was setting behind the Moab Rim, and the cumulus clouds on the western horizon were dark purple against a light blue sky, their edges glowing with a bright orange iridescence. He always took a few moments to enjoy high-desert sunsets. Each evening was an opportunity for mother nature to show off to the world what she could do. When he was a little boy, his grandmother told him that all sunsets were different. No two alike. Each was beautiful in its own way. They were daily messages from God reminding little boys and girls that He existed, that He was watching them, and that He was there to help them whenever life got tough. He stared at the display for a few minutes, then got into his pickup and headed home. He would resume his investigation in the morning.

14

AFTER BREAKFAST AT the Rim Rock Diner, Rivera swung by the office, grabbed a mug of coffee, and checked his messages finding nothing urgent. He called Lucas Nichols and made an appointment to visit him at his ranch. Rivera had never met the man in person and knew him only by reputation. He'd moved from California to Moab about two years ago and bought an expensive condo in town and a 600-acre ranch which fronted Hwy 128 near Hittle Bottom. He'd spent a career in Hollywood as a movie producer and word had it that he retired quite wealthy. He had a particular interest in Southwest history and had produced an award-winning series of documentaries describing the lives of key figures in its exploration and settlement. He was known to be a generous donor to history museums and related historical associations.

Rivera drove upriver on Hwy 128 into the morning sun. The red rock cliffs that bordered the river were corrugated with vertical shadows, and a V-shaped formation of geese flew overhead. A lone kayaker paddling downriver waved to him and he returned the greeting.

He turned into the ranch entrance and rattled across a cattle guard onto a gravel road. As far as he could see, the brush-covered terrain was devoid of livestock. Evidently, the new owner hadn't bought the ranch to raise cattle.

Fifty yards off to his right, he saw a cluster of dilapidated buildings. He pulled to a stop and studied the structures, guessing they formed the ghost town he observed in Derek Webster's video where the diggings were taking place.

He continued driving up a long grade until the road ended at a Spanish style home with tan stucco walls and a red tile roof. It was surrounded by a three-foot high wall plastered with stucco that matched the house. The yard consisted of red-rock gravel populated with a sprinkling of agaves and yuccas. He parked and walked toward the house, noting the impressive view of the river. Lucas Nichols came out of the house and greeted Rivera with a handshake.

"Welcome Deputy Rivera." He was a tall man with a handsome face, dark wavy hair with traces of gray, and a Hollywood smile. Rivera guessed his age to be about sixty.

"Thanks for seeing me on such short notice, Mr. Nichols."

"Sure, Deputy. What's this about?"

"I understand you've been having some trouble with damage to your property."

"Well, that's true, but I haven't reported it to the police." Nichols looked confused. "How did you find out about it?"

"I'm investigating the death of Derek Webster. You hired him to surveil that old ghost town on your property."

Nichols's face froze. "Derek's dead?"

"Yes. He was shot in the back yesterday. Up in the mountains."

"I didn't know that. I don't get much news when I'm staying out here on the ranch. What happened? Was it an accident?"

"That's what I'm trying to find out."

"You mean it might have been intentional?"

"We don't know. The investigation is just getting started."

"I can't imagine why anyone would shoot Derek deliberately. He seemed like a fine human being."

"How did you learn about Derek and his drone business?"

"Through a hunting acquaintance by the name of Billy Blevins. He told me how Derek helped him locate a bull elk in the mountains. I was kind of shocked. I do a little hunting myself, but I'd never resort to anything like that. Doesn't seem fair. But it gave me an idea about how to find out who's been damaging my property."

"What kind of damage?"

"Well, it's really not a big deal. It's more of an annoyance than real damage. Probably not worth your time. But if you'd like, we could go there, and I'll show you what's been going on."

"Let's have a look."

They hopped into Rivera's vehicle and drove back toward the entry.

"This is a beautiful place you have here."

"Thanks, I have big plans for it." Nichols pointed. "Turn left here."

Rivera turned onto a two-track leading to the cluster of old buildings he'd observed as he drove in.

"I've been reluctant to get law enforcement involved in this," said Nichols. "I believe the digging is being done by young kids and I really don't want them to get in trouble. I thought maybe I could solve the problem myself. You know, find out who they are and talk to their parents."

Rivera parked a short distance from the building complex. They got out of his vehicle and walked around the remains of old wooden buildings that once formed a tiny community. There were twelve of them, fifteen if you counted the small sheds. The larger buildings had two or three rooms, and the smaller ones were simple one-room structures. The walls consisted of vertical wood planks, some of which were broken, warped, or had fallen off. The roofs were corrugated metal, rusted and damaged by wind and time. Behind the buildings was a tiny spring which created a small pool of water and attracted birds and other critters in search of a drink. Farther back was a small cemetery with a few wooden grave markers, now weather worn and broken. The one-time community wreaked of history.

Nichols pointed to some holes which had been dug into the ground between the buildings. There were eleven of them, each about two feet in diameter and a foot deep. Inside the buildings where the wood floors had rotted away were more holes.

"I don't know why they're doing this," he said as they entered one of the buildings. Maybe they think they'll find some kind of treasure. Besides digging these holes, they also made off with some iron skillets and utensils that were here."

"I recognized one of the boys from Derek's video footage. I'll pay him and his folks a visit. You shouldn't have any more trouble."

"I appreciate that. And lest you think I'm making a big fuss over nothing, my intention when I bought this ranch was to build a small museum dedicated to Utah ghost towns. There are hundreds of them like this one scattered all over the state. Most are related to mining ventures or water stops for the railroads back when locomotives were powered by steam. Besides the main museum building, I'll fix up this broken-down collection of buildings and let it serve as an example of how adventuresome people lived back in those days. It's important that we not forget what this country was like and how the pioneers lived before the tourists with their Jeeps and cell phones got here. I'm doing research now on the history of this place. It was once the base for exploration activities by men searching for gold in the LaSal Mountains."

"A museum is a great idea."

"My hope is that the museum will attract researchers interested in ghost towns and the history of southeast Utah. I've got a long way to go, and I plan to start soon."

They drove back to the house. Rivera shook hands with Nichols. "I'll get back to you after I talk to the boy and his parents."

"Thank you. I appreciate it."

15

RIVERA DROVE DIRECTLY to the Smith residence. He parked and rang the doorbell. David Smith, his long-time neighbor, opened the door. He was about forty with curly auburn hair and a young face. He was wearing one of the official Moab uniforms—T-shirt, shorts, and trail shoes. He and Rivera had been friends since the day Rivera moved to Moab. Smith had loaned the deputy some tools back then so he could repair a loose screen on his front door.

Smith smiled. "Hi, Manny. What's up?"

"Dave, I need to talk to you about something Stewart's been up to."

The smile faded from Smith's face. "Oh hell, what's that boy done now?" He gestured Rivera into the house. They sat in the living room, Smith leaning forward in his chair.

"What'd he do?"

"I don't think this is a big problem, Dave, but it needs to be handled right."

Rivera explained the story to the father, describing the recently purchased ranch at Hittle Bottom, the ghost town complex surrounded by a barbed wire fence, the holes that were dug, and the missing skillets and utensils. He left out the part about Derek Webster's death and his drone business. "Dave, the owner's name is Lucas Nichols. All he wants is for the vandalism to stop. He plans on converting that collection of old buildings into part of a historical museum featuring Utah's ghost towns, and he doesn't want any further damage to the property."

Just then, the front door opened, and Stewart bounded in. He was a miniature of his father with curly hair and freckles. He was wearing threadbare jeans and a faded purple T-shirt and looked to be about fourteen years old. He stopped when he saw Rivera.

Dave stood up, walked over to the boy, took him by the arm, and led him to the couch. "Stewart, sit down and tell us what you've been doing at the Nichols Ranch."

"The boy sat, produced a look of innocence, and turned his palms up. "What do you mean, Dad?"

"Don't play games with me, Son. You know perfectly well what I mean. I'm talking about the holes you and your friends have been digging at that ghost town on private property."

The boy shrugged. "Ronnie said it was BLM land. I didn't know we were on someone's ranch."

"You and Ronnie Stokes and who else? There were three of you."

"Me and Ronnie and Doug Ferguson. Ronnie told us there were lots of old ghost towns in Utah and his father had some books on them. Ronnie read all about them. He said some of those ghost towns were set up by men in search of gold. We figured that maybe they left some behind, you know, like small pieces that were accidentally dropped. He said we should check a few of them out and see what we could find. We got all excited. Ronnie borrowed his father's metal detector and off we went. We visited several of them and looked around but didn't find anything interesting. All we detected were nails and bits of metal. No gold. At the Hittle Bottom ruins, we didn't find any gold, but we found some old cooking pots and utensils in one of the buildings."

His father sat back, a mixture of relief and embarrassment on his face. "Where are the pots and utensils?"

"Ronnie's got them. Honest, we didn't know we were on private property."

"You climbed through a barbed-wire fence, didn't you?"

"Sure, but we thought it was all public land."

"Well, the three of you are going with me to visit Mr. Nichols tomorrow morning. You are going to return what you took, fill in the holes you dug, and apologize to Mr. Nichols for what you did."

"Yes, Sir."

Rivera stood up, trying to keep the smile off his face. He said goodbye and went to his car. While he was sitting in the vehicle thinking about his next move, Dave Smith came rushing out of the house. Rivera lowered his window.

"Manny, is my boy going to have a record because of this?"

"No, Dave. I'll leave the matter in your hands. The boys' names won't be mentioned in my report. I'll call Mr. Nichols and tell him to expect to hear from you."

As Rivera drove off, he reflected on some of the silly things he and his friends had done when he was Stewart's age. There was the time they stole the milk the delivery man had left at Mrs. Ashwalt's back door so they could feed a couple of stray cats they'd found. And the time his friend Willie secretly borrowed his father's car keys so they could drive his car around the block without permission, and how that ended up with a wrinkled right front fender because of an unfortunately placed telephone pole. And the time he and Willie and Bob, all faithful altar boys, snuck into St. Paul's Catholic Church when they thought no one was there, tiptoed into the sacristy, and drank some of the wine. And how the priest caught them as they were leaving. He could go on and on. He was thankful no one had ever filed a complaint with the police for some of the missteps of his youth.

16

RIVERA'S NEXT STEP was to pay a visit to Phil Broderick, the private investigator who had been one of Derek Webster's clients. He lived in Spanish Valley in a development called Rim Village, a community of Spanish-style, four-plex condos south of town. Rivera drove to the subdivision and located Broderick's condo. An old, white Ford F-150 with scratches on the sides and a rusty dent in the front fender was parked in the driveway. The patio was fenced with a four-foot-high adobe wall, and a Kokopelli sculpture was welded to the front gate. He entered the patio and rang the doorbell.

The door opened and Rivera saw an older man with a sagging face, a bald head, and a generous girth standing there. He was wearing khaki slacks and a baggy white shirt with the shirttails hanging out. The stub of a cigar protruded from his mouth. Rivera introduced himself and said he had some questions he'd like to ask. Broderick pulled the door open and invited him to come inside. The place looked like a bachelor pad that needed a good cleaning. The living room was comfortably furnished but sparsely decorated, and the smell of cigar smoke permeated the air.

A small bulldog trotted out of a back room, gave Rivera's pant leg a couple of sniffs, and stood there looking up at the deputy. Rivera had heard of people who look like their dogs, but this was the first time he'd seen it in real life. The dog's pronounced jowls and the bags under its eyes made it a dead ringer for Broderick. It was all Rivera could do to keep from laughing.

"Have a seat," said Broderick, gesturing with his cigar toward a brown couch.

Rivera sat down.

"You look familiar," said Broderick. "Haven't we met somewhere?" He stabbed his cigar back into his mouth and grunted as he lowered his bulk into an overstuffed chair.

Rivera reminded him that they'd met briefly at a fund raiser at the Lions Club.

"Ah, yes, I remember now. You weren't wearing your uniform that evening. Well, how can I help you today?"

"Have you heard about the shooting death of Derek Webster?"

"Of course. It's been all over the news."

"You're in the private investigations business, aren't you?"

"I had a practice in Grand Junction for thirty years. Then I retired and moved here. I still take on projects now and then, but I'm mostly retired."

"I understand Derek was doing some work for you."

Broderick leaned back, extracted a lighter from his pants pocket, and relit his cigar. He thought for a long moment before responding. "Yes, that's true. He was helping me with one of my investigations. What about it?"

"I'm investigating his death. I'm trying to learn as much as I can about him. What was the nature of the work he was doing for you?"

"Wait. Are you saying that someone intentionally killed him? I'd understood it was a hunting accident."

"It might have been. We just don't know yet. But as I'm sure you're aware, an investigation is required in any shooting death." Rivera tried to make the tone of his response sound matter of fact. He had no desire to reveal his strong suspicion that Derek was murdered. "So, back to my question. What was the nature of the work he was doing for you?"

"Well, I can't get into specifics because of client confidentiality—you know that—but he's done some aerial reconnaissance work for me with his drones. His drones can go places and see things that would be difficult if not impossible for me to pull off. I can't tell you much more than that. The ethics of my profession prohibits me from naming names or going into detail."

Rivera decided not to let on that he already knew the nature of the work and the identities of the parties involved. "Is it possible the work he was doing for you might have given someone a motive to kill him?"

"Sure, anything's possible. But I doubt it. His assignment involved a matter of, shall we say, a family situation. It's a possible motive for murder, but not a likely one in this particular case. That's just my opinion, of course. I don't really have any way of knowing."

"I've been checked out on the equipment in his vehicle and also in his lab. Could you tell me how you communicated with him? How you retained him, how he transmitted surveillance videos to you, and so forth? How did all that work?"

"What lab? I didn't know he had a lab."

"He had a well-equipped lab in a storage unit he rented. It's full of electronic equipment and drones."

"I'll be damned. I didn't know that. I thought all his equipment was housed in that vehicle of his." Broderick thought for a moment. "I should have figured that out. I'm a damn PI. I'm supposed to observe and deduce." He shook his head. "I never picked up on that. I guess I'm getting old."

"How did you first retain him?"

"I heard about his capabilities from a guy who's a volunteer with the Grand County Search and Rescue program. He told me he'd heard that Derek might be interested in taking on some paying jobs, so I contacted him and asked him if he was interested. He said yes. I asked him if he could demonstrate his capabilities to

me and he said he would do that. He left and I didn't
hear from him for a couple of days. Then, one morning,
he knocked on my door and handed me a thumb drive.
He said I might be interested in the video it contained.
I plugged it into my computer and played it. It showed
me leaving my condo, getting into my pickup, driving
into town, and entering City Market. Then it showed me
leaving the store, loading up my groceries, and returning
home. I never saw or heard the drone. It even caught me
scratching my ass one time when I thought no one was
looking. I had to laugh. At that moment, I was sold on
the guy."

"You decided you could use his services."

"Sure I did. I only wish I had that capability when I
was doing PI work back in Grand Junction." He rubbed
his hands together and squirmed in his seat, warming up
to the topic. He was almost licking his chops. "Think of
the possibilities, man. I could have implanted monitors
in otherwise inaccessible places. Listening devices,
transmitters, recorders, video cameras, whatever.
Anything I wanted placed anywhere a drone could fly."
He grinned and pounded his knee with his fist. "Damn,
just think of that."

"So you hired him."

"Right. I had one open case where surveillance in the
mountains was needed. I'm not much for hiking in the
woods anymore, so his drone seemed like the perfect
solution."

"Did it work out well?"

Broderick removed the cigar stub from his mouth, looked at it, and relit it. "It's still an open investigation, but so far, it's been very helpful."

"Did you go to Derek's cabana to view the videos?"

"No. He transferred each video to a thumb drive for me. I picked up the thumb drive and took it home. I played it back on my computer."

Rivera decided to push one last time. "Are you sure you can't tell me what he was working on? It might shed some light on the reason for his death."

"I wish I could. But if I violate a confidence, I might lose my license."

Rivera sensed the interview was at a dead end. He probed Broderick with a few more general questions about the case but received nothing more than vague responses. The deputy decided there was no point in pressing him any longer since he already knew the parties involved and the matter of infidelity. He thanked the man and left.

He decided to visit Ginny Hempstead next, the woman who, according to Derek's notes, hired Broderick in the first place. If there was anything important or unusual about the work Broderick was doing for her, she might be willing to share it.

17

RIVERA HAD NEVER met Ginny Hempstead but knew her by reputation. She was a wealthy fiftyish woman who was involved in several charitable organizations in Moab and gave generously to help them. She was particularly supportive of the Moab Home for Needy Children and Mrs. Densford's Home for the Elderly. Her husband Carl had passed away four years ago after a long bout with leukemia. Then, last year, after a brief courtship, she married Gene Squires, a younger man, a man most everyone in town knew was a gigolo. If the town gossips had the story straight, Ginny knew of his sullied reputation when she married him, but she'd been lonely living by herself in a big house and decided to marry him anyway. And, of course, most everyone who knew Gene Squires believed his true objective was an easy life using her money.

Rivera called Ginny, learned she was available now, and set up a visit. He drove south out of Moab to a gated community called Navajo Ridge set in the foothills of the mountains. At the front gate, he punched in the entry code she'd given him and continued on a road winding up to the edge of a cliff overlooking Mill Creek. He parked in the driveway of a sprawling two-story rock house, a mansion by Moab standards. The doorbell produced a pleasant series of chimes.

A slender woman wearing designer slacks and a long-sleeve yellow top opened the door. Her hair was light brown with blonde highlights. Everything about the woman and her residence suggested wealth.

"Come in, Deputy Rivera." She extended her hand. "I'm Ginny Hempstead."

She struck Rivera as a polished, intelligent woman. He shook her hand and thanked her for seeing him.

"Let's go into the living room and sit down."

The living room was large, and the interior looked like it had been designed by a professional. The furniture looked expensive, and a massive oriental rug covered the floor. Huge windows provided a spectacular view of Mill Creek Canyon.

She smiled, but it was a cautious smile. "How can I help you, Deputy?"

"I'm investigating the shooting that took place in the mountains yesterday. Have you heard about it?"

"Yes, I have. What a terrible shame."

"The man who was shot was assisting Phil Broderick on an investigation. I believe the investigation was being conducted on your behalf." He raised his eyebrows, converting the statement into a question.

"Would you like some coffee?"

"I'd love some."

She got up, left the room, and returned a few minutes later with a coffee service for two, fancy napkins, and a plate of chocolate chip cookies. She placed the tray on the coffee table in front of Rivera and filled the cups with coffee.

He took a sip. "Delicious. Thank you."

"May I assume this conversation will be held in the utmost confidence?"

"I can't guarantee that, but I'll do my best."

She stared at Rivera and thought for a long moment. "Aren't you the deputy who placed that ad in the local newspaper a few days before the last election? The one that caused Denny Campbell to lose the election for sheriff?"

The memories of that stressful time came tumbling back in Rivera's mind. Campbell had been running for sheriff against the incumbent Louise Anderson, trying to reclaim the job he'd lost to her in the previous election. There was bad blood between Rivera and Campbell, a result of Campbell's incompetence, dishonesty, and arrogance. The man spent more time on the golf course with his buddies then he did in the office. Things had become so strained between them that, one time, Rivera had come close to slugging Campbell. Because of a wealthy man's disdain for Sheriff Louise Anderson, the result of her mistakenly arresting him, he threw his support and substantial resources behind Campbell's election campaign. As a result, the polls had Campbell several percentage points ahead a week before the election. It looked like he was going to win. Rivera knew he could never work for Campbell again, so he took one last shot. He was aware the people of Grand County had a high regard for him, so he ran an ad in the local newspaper a few days before the election stating that he believed Anderson was a much better choice for sheriff, and that if Campbell won the election, he would resign. It was a tough decision and Rivera knew he'd have to leave the town he loved to find a new job if Campbell won. Fortunately, Campbell lost the election and Rivera's life in Moab continued as he had hoped. Afterwards, Campbell had threatened to get even, but so far, he had not taken any action.

"Yeah. That was me."

"That took a lot of guts. I knew Campbell. He wasn't very bright. And he spent too many of his working hours goofing off around town. He asked me out a couple of times after my husband Carl passed away." She laughed. "Fat chance I would have dated him. I didn't know you at the time, but I was always impressed with what you did. You took a big chance and saved the community from what I believe would have been a bad situation. You say you'll do your utmost to keep our conversation in confidence?"

"To the best of my ability, yes."

"After what you did for the people of Grand County, I believe I can trust you."

Rivera took another sip of coffee and waited.

"About your question, yes, I hired Phil Broderick. I hired him to tail my husband." She frowned and pointed to a framed photograph of a handsome man with dark curly hair and a roguish smile, the same man Rivera had seen in the video. "That's my new husband Gene Squires. We've been married for about a year. He's a cheat and a scoundrel. I keep his photograph on display to remind myself of how stupid I was to marry him, and so he doesn't realize that I'm about to divorce him. After all, he still lives here. He won't be back for another three or four hours, so we have time to talk. Today is Thursday, one of his dalliance days with that blonde floozie he's been seeing for the last couple of months. His cover story is that he goes hiking with some guys he met in the Sierra Club."

Rivera felt confused. "It's a personal matter, I guess, but I'm curious. Why are you waiting to divorce him?" He picked up a cookie, bit off a piece, and chewed it as she responded.

"It has to do with our prenuptial agreement. Carl left me pretty well off when he passed away. He was a good man who had a successful career on Wall Street as a bond trader. After he was gone, I missed him terribly. I just about couldn't stand it. Then Gene Squires came into my life. He was kind of cute and I was very lonely. We started spending a lot of time together and eventually got married. I know he married me for my money—after all, I'm eighteen years older than he is—but I didn't expect all this cheating that's been going on. Anyway, my attorney put language in our prenup to the effect that, in the event of a divorce, infidelity, among other things, would result in his having no claim whatsoever on my wealth."

"So Broderick is supposed to get you proof of infidelity that will stand up in a court of law."

"That's correct. Phil hired that drone fellow to help him document the infidelity. I'm paying Phil two thousand a week until the job is done. Fortunately, money is not a problem for me."

"Did you see the results of the videos he recorded?"

"Yes, he showed me a couple of them. We saw them meeting and hiking into the woods several times, but we haven't caught them in the act yet, if you know what I mean. My attorney says I need *incontrovertible* proof of his infidelity."

Rivera figured he had all the information he needed for now. He finished his coffee and stood up. "Thanks for your time. I'll do everything possible to keep this in confidence. I don't want to jeopardize your legal case."

Ginny got up. "I appreciate that."

"By the way, I want you to know that Phil Broderick didn't give me your name or share with me the details of your investigation. He said he wouldn't violate a confidence. I got the information from the drone operator's handwritten records and videos."

"I'm glad to hear that."

Rivera walked to the front door and opened it. He stopped. It occurred to him that Gene Squires might have had a motive to kill Derek Webster. If Squires became aware that a drone was recording his activities, he might have decided to eliminate the drone operator to protect his claim on the Hempstead fortune.

"I've never met Gene Squires. Do you think he's the type that's capable of murder?"

She laughed. "God, no. I don't think he's got the guts. He's just a pretty boy." Then the grin on her face faded. "But I guess there's no telling what some people might do for money."

18

RIVERA'S NEXT STEP in his investigation was a visit to the home of Sam Stickle, a rancher who lived in Spanish Valley and moved his herd of cattle from the valley to the LaSal Mountains for better grazing during the summer months. Sam was the father of Rivera's next-door neighbor and the grandfather of the young boy the deputy often spent time with, throwing a football back and forth between their front lawns. Rivera had been friends with Sam since he'd first rented his house in Moab. The deputy had often been invited to the Stickle home for dinner. Sam was an influential and highly respected rancher, well known throughout southeast Utah. He was considered a leader by the other ranchers. Rivera was sure Sam would know something about Eddie and the group of ranchers who had hired Derek to chase down wolves.

As Rivera drove out of Navajo Ridge and headed for Sam's place, his cell phone buzzed. The caller was Deputy Sheriff Emmett Mitchell.

"Manny, you asked me to call you if there were any new developments involving peyote in San Juan County. I never expected to hear anything but, as it turns out, there's been a recent incident. The administrator of the Blue Mountain Hospital here in Blanding called me a little while ago. He said a very sick eighteen-year-old girl from Monticello by the name of Abigail Nolan was checked into the hospital earlier today by her parents. Her symptoms were dilated pupils, increased heart rate, and excessive sweating. They were worried because the daughter confessed she'd experimented with peyote with some of her college friends. She said it only happened this one time. She was just curious about it. The doctor said she was suffering from a temporary psychosis and should be fine after the mescaline wears off."

"Did she say where she got it?"

"I plan to visit her later and ask that question. I want to give her time for the drug to wear off. You're welcome to join me."

"Thanks, Emmett. Let me know when you set up a visit."

"Will do."

Rivera clicked off. Now he had a bit of a dilemma. Should he relay the information to the DEA right away? Or should he wait until Emmett gathers more information? And should he accompany Emmett when he visits the girl? He remembered Sheriff Anderson's comments about DEA Agent Masters and her clear admonition: *Stay out of it.* But if he could find an answer for Lucia Navarro's father about where his daughter had gotten the peyote, it might give the man some peace of mind. At least he would know that an investigation was taking place, and that his daughter's death wasn't being ignored by the authorities. Rivera wasn't sure what he should do. He finally decided to just wait for Emmett's call and discuss the matter with him. Then he'd decide what to do.

Rivera drove through the front gate of Sam Stickle's property and parked in front of the barn where he saw Sam tinkering with an ancient John Deere tractor. After his family and ranching, rebuilding old farm machinery was Sam's love. He waved when he spotted Rivera and walked over to greet him. He was a stocky man wearing bib overalls and a plaid shirt with the sleeves rolled up, exposing massive forearms. He had a round face and a salt-and-pepper buzz cut. Rivera considered him to be a salt-of-the-earth, hardworking, honest man and a credit to the community, but whenever Rivera shook hands with him, it was always with trepidation. Stickle had the strongest grip of any man Rivera had ever met. He didn't know his own strength.

"Welcome, Manny. Nice to see you." He smiled, pulled a rag from his back pocket, and wiped his hands. He extended a meaty, calloused hand in Rivera's direction.

Rivera looked at Sam's hand, smiled, and shook it. Today it was firm but gentle. The deputy relaxed.

"What brings you out this way," asked Sam.

"I came here to ask you about a delicate matter."

Sam's smile faded. "What's that?"

"Have you heard about the wolves in the LaSals?"

He gave Rivera a long stare. "Sure I have. What about them?"

"Do you have any of your herd up in the mountains now?"

"Part of it. I brought most of them down over the past two weeks and I'll move the rest during the next week or so. We're moving them out of the mountains now because the nights up there are starting to get cold, and the good grass is pretty much played out. Rounding them up in the mountains is time-consuming. You almost have to chase them down one by one. And when a calf gets separated from its mother, it's even more of a challenge."

Rivera nodded, thinking how best to phrase his next question. "Are you worried about wolves killing your cattle?"

Another long stare. "Well sure, but I haven't lost any yet. At least none I'm aware of."

"I assume all the ranchers are concerned."

Sam frowned. "You know, Manny, we've known each other for a lot of years. It's not like you to be beating around the bush like this. Why don't you just tell me what's on your mind?"

"You're right, Sam. It's just that you're a rancher, and I've learned that some of the ranchers have banded together to kill off the wolves in the LaSals, and I don't know if you're part of the group. That makes it awkward for me because I want to ask you if you know who's in charge of the group."

"I'm not part of the group. At least not yet. I've been invited to join but so far, I haven't made a decision. And don't bother telling me it's against the law. I know all about the Endangered Species Act. But my opinion is that there are plenty of wolves in North America. They don't need any special protection."

"I'm pretty sure the point man of the group is a guy named Eddie. I don't have his last name and I don't know any Eddies in the ranching community. But I'd like to talk with him. My concern is not so much about protecting wolves. I'll leave that to the feds. It's about the killing of Derek Webster in the mountains yesterday. There may be an indirect connection between the two."

Sam thought for a long moment. "Well, I'm not going to tell you who he is. If I did, I'd lose every friend I've got in the ranching community. But I'll tell you what I will do. I'll get word to him and see if he's willing to talk to you. That's the best I can do."

"Fair enough, Sam. Thanks for the help."

19

RIVERA DROVE BACK to the office and grabbed a mug of coffee from the break room. He closed his office door and sat down. His in-basket contained a report from the Medical Examiner which he picked up and scanned. It added nothing to what he already knew. Derek Webster died from a bullet to the back. Except for his prosthetic feet, he'd been an otherwise healthy man. Attached to the report was a transparent evidence bag containing the bullet extracted from the victim.

Rivera had some thinking to do about his case, but first there was one item he wanted to wrap up. He picked up the phone and called Lucas Nichols.

"Mr. Nichols, I've talked with the father of one of the boys who have been vandalizing your property. I don't think you'll be having any more trouble with them."

"Thanks for getting back to me. Yes, I know. David Smith called me. He'll be bringing the three boys out here tomorrow to repair the damage to the ghost town and return the items they took. And as I told you, I'm not interested in pressing charges."

"Good. We've all done silly things at that age."

Nichols laughed. "I know I have. I'd be too embarrassed to mention some of the crazy stunts I pulled as a kid. Thanks for your help, Deputy."

That done, Rivera could now scratch the Nichols Ranch diggings off his list of possible motives for killing Derek Webster. No one involved had anything to gain from his death. Rivera now had only two remaining possibilities, the work being done for the private investigator, and the effort by the local ranchers to eliminate the wolf threat.

The phone on his desk rang. The caller identified himself simply as Eddie, withholding his last name. He had a deep, gruff voice and sounded like a man who was sure of himself.

"Sam Stickle said you wanted to talk to me."

"That's right. Thanks for the call. I'm investigating the shooting of Derek Webster in the mountains yesterday. You were a client of his. What can you tell me about what he was doing for you?"

There was a long pause. "I'm not breaking any laws. I represent a group of ranchers concerned about the wolves that were released in the mountains. My job is to search for them and if I spot one, report its location to my clients. The ranchers take it from there. I hired Webster to help with the search. I was paying him to spot wolves for me."

"So they could be eliminated."

"I suppose. What the ranchers do after I find the wolves is none of my business. But my opinion is that the people who released the wolves in the mountains had no business doing that. That's not the kind of thing you just suddenly spring on a community without first having public meetings and discussions."

Rivera noted the implied assertion that Eddie's job didn't include killing the wolves he located. The deputy wasn't so sure he believed that. "When did you start working for the ranchers?"

"A couple of days after that notice about the wolf release was published in the newspaper."

"How did you get involved in this?"

"I'm what is known as a problem solver. A fixer. It's my occupation. I take on the kind of jobs nobody wants. Unpleasant jobs. Dirty jobs. Sometimes dangerous jobs. My job in this case is to solve the wolf problem. I was hired by people who wish to remain nameless."

"Have you learned the identity of the people who released the wolves?"

"I have an idea who might be behind it, but I'm not certain."

"Mind telling me who you suspect?"

"I guess not. If it helps find the creep who shot Derek, that's a good thing. Derek reminded me of some of the guys I fought with when I was in the Special Forces—guys who got badly wounded or permanently handicapped, but who pushed on through life anyway. I didn't know him well, but in the short time we were acquainted, I developed a lot of respect for him, given how well he rebuilt his life after the accident that cost him his feet. Howard Hollingdale is a guy who might be behind the wolf release. He's an environmentalist who wants all government owned land to be returned to its original state. That means no timber harvesting, no mining, no oil or gas wells, and certainly no cattle. I have no firsthand knowledge of who's behind the wolf release, but if he's not the one, I'll bet he knows who is."

"I'm not familiar with the name. Where does he live?"

"Monticello."

"Do you think the friction between the environmental activists and the ranchers is intense enough that someone might have decided to eliminate Derek's drones from the equation in order to protect the wolves?"

"That's possible, but it wouldn't make a lot of sense. Derek wasn't the only guy in the drone business. I've already hired a couple of brothers in Grand Junction to replace him. They have the same types of drones that Derek used. They're going to be picking up for me where Derek left off. And if need be, there are others I can hire. It seems unlikely to me that the killer would just keep killing drone operators."

That logic struck a chord with Rivera, but it was possible a man whose wolves were threatened might not think it through that same way. "Well, thank you. I appreciate the help. If I have any more questions, is there a number where I can reach you?" Rivera figured he wouldn't get a straight answer. Eddie was probably calling from a public phone.

He heard a chuckle. "I don't give out that kind of information. If one of the enviros gets mad enough, I could be the next target. You can get in touch with me through Sam Stickle. Same way you did this time."

Eddie clicked off, leaving Rivera sitting there listening to a dial tone. He dropped the phone into its cradle and looked at his watch. Six-thirty. He decided to call it a day and visit Hollingdale in the morning.

On the way home, he picked up a pizza with sausage and mushrooms for dinner. After feeding the guppies and his dog Bentley, he sat at the kitchen table eating the pizza and thinking about the Derek Webster case. He hoped his investigation was on the right track, but it was too soon to know for sure.

He finished the pizza, washed it down with a cold beer, and grabbed a second one. He went outside into his backyard, Bentley tagging along behind him. He settled into one of the two canvas lawn chairs in the middle of the yard and stared into the gathering darkness enveloping the LaSal Mountains. A full moon was barely visible over the peaks. He sat there, staring at it, watching it rise higher and higher in slow motion while he stroked the top of Bentley's head. His thoughts turned to Gloria. She loved to watch the moon rise. He pulled his cell phone from his shirt pocket and called her number.

She answered on the second ring. "Hi, Honey."

"Hi, Sweetheart. I'm sitting in the backyard with Bentley. You should be here. There's a full moon rising over the mountains."

"Oh, I love that. I wish I was there. How are you doing?"

"I'm fine. Still working on the Derek Webster case."

"How's that going?"

"Pretty slow. I'm chasing down a few leads but no real progress yet."

"I'm sure you'll figure it out. You always do."

They talked for twenty more minutes about a wide range of topics: his family in Las Cruces, her parents in Española, her BLM training program, his work, the weather, Moab, and so forth.

After they said, "I love you," and hung up, Rivera missed her even more. She sounded happy, even more than usual. Could a BLM training program be that enjoyable? She went for several months without a job after she moved to Moab as his wife. Maybe she had missed having a job more than Rivera realized. Or maybe she was just enjoying the company of her fellow trainees studying to become BLM agents. Either way, Rivera felt a touch of jealousy knowing that she was happy and having fun without him. He examined his feelings. Was he disappointed she could be happy despite being away from him? Or was he just lonely, his life having reverted to the way it was in his bachelor days? He wasn't sure.

20

RIVERA ARRIVED AT the office the next morning and called Emmett Mitchell. It was a courtesy call to inform him that he would be driving down to San Juan County to interview one of its residents, Howard Hollingdale.

"Morning, Emmett."

"Hey Manny, I was just getting ready to call you. I'm planning to visit Abigail Nolan and her parents this morning. The symptoms she experienced from using peyote have subsided for the most part, and she's doing much better. I want to find out where she got the stuff. Care to join me?"

Rivera thought about that. His instructions from Sheriff Anderson were to steer clear of the peyote business. That was understood. But that order related to the peyote case in Grand County. This was a different peyote case in a different county. Rivera knew he was rationalizing but couldn't resist the opportunity to satisfy his curiosity. And perhaps he would learn something he could privately share with Emiliano Navarro about Lucia's death—something that would satisfy the man's need to believe that law enforcement was indeed conducting an investigation. If that would soften his grief, then, to Rivera, it might be worth the risk of getting chewed out.

"Yeah, count me in. I'd like to hear what she has to say. I'll probably get in trouble for this, but I want to know more about this sudden appearance of illegal peyote in the community. If the DEA asks me why I was meddling in something I was told to stay away from, I'll just blame it on you."

Mitchell laughed. "Meet me at the Nolan residence in Blanding in two hours." He gave Rivera the address.

"Okay. Now I've got one for you. Do you know a guy by the name of Howard Hollingdale? I need to ask him a few questions about wolves."

"Sure. He's one of our more prominent citizens. He lives in Monticello. He's a noted environmentalist. Lots of books, publications, TV appearances, so forth. He's a good citizen and very intelligent. And he enjoys a good debate and getting under his opponent's skin. He'll have a man of limited intelligence like yourself for lunch."

Rivera smiled. "I guess I'll just have to take my chances."

"What's your interest in him?"

Rivera explained that Derek Webster had been doing drone surveillance in the LaSals looking for wolves on behalf of a consortium of ranchers who graze their cattle in the mountains during the summer months. "It's the intent of the ranchers to capture or kill the wolves released there a few weeks ago by a group called *Restore the Wolves.* I'm thinking it's possible some radical environmentalist struck back by killing the drone operator."

"Wow, that's really a long shot. I know how thorough you are about chasing down every lead, but that seems pretty unlikely."

"I know, but it's something I need to check out." Rivera thought back on the sage advice his old boss gave him. Sheriff Leroy Bradshaw, his mentor during his early years of conducting investigations, taught him that every lead must be thoroughly checked out until the investigator understands completely what happened, why it happened, and how the sequence of events unfolded. Absent that, the investigator might make a false assumption about what happened and why, leading him down the wrong logical path to an incorrect conclusion, a trap Rivera always did his best to avoid.

"Okay," said Mitchell, "I'll see you at the Nolan residence at ten o'clock."

Rivera called Millie Ives, the dispatcher, and briefed her on his plans. He stated his purpose was to follow up on a lead related to the wolves being released in the mountains. He omitted any mention of his peyote interest and felt guilty for doing so. Not only was Millie the Grand County dispatcher for longer than anyone could remember, but she had also become a close friend of Rivera's over the years. After Chris Carey's wife passed away, Rivera had managed to bring Chris and Millie together as a couple. Rivera hoped he wasn't risking his friendship with her by not being totally forthcoming regarding the purpose of his trip.

Before leaving his office, Rivera called Guy Richardson on his cell phone. He wanted to be sure Hal Webster was okay. The foreman answered on the first ring.

"Hi Deputy Rivera."

"Hi, Guy. I was just calling to check on Hal. How's he doing?"

"Not well. I've never seen anyone so depressed. He just sits on the porch all day long, wrapped in a blanket, rocking back and forth. If I didn't make him eat, I believe he'd starve to death."

"It must be a terrible loss for him."

"Yeah. Hal doesn't say much about it, but yesterday evening he opened up a little bit. All he could say was that he'd never get over losing Derek. He was crying. He gestured toward the greenhouses and said, 'What was the point of building all this? My life is over.'"

"Anything I can do?"

"No. Hopefully the passage of time will help heal his wounds. Thanks for calling."

Rivera sat there for a long time, reflecting on the sadness of the situation. He wished there was a way he could help Hal with his grief, but there was nothing he could do to bring Derek back. All that was in his power was to identify the killer and lock him up. And sitting in his office feeling bad for Hal wasn't helping to accomplish that goal.

As Rivera exited his office, he ran into Sheriff Anderson in the hallway.

"Anything new on the Derek Webster case?"

"No. Just a bunch of loose ends I need to chase down. Hopefully one of them will pan out."

"We're starting to get calls from the hunting community. They're asking if it's safe to go into the mountains. The Times-Independent is doing a feature story on the life and death of Derek. Turns out he's kind of a cult figure in the hiking world. The article is sure to stir up the pot, keep away visitors, and hurt the business community. We don't need that. So let's solve this case as soon as possible. And keep me posted."

"Will do."

Rivera left the building, hopped into his vehicle, and headed south toward Blanding, hoping he wasn't about to get himself in big trouble.

21

RIVERA FOUND THE Nolan home on a cul de sac at the end of a residential street shaded with cottonwood trees. Emmett Mitchell's unit was parked in front of the house, a white clapboard structure with blue shutters and a well-tended yard. Mitchell got out of his pickup as Rivera parked behind him.

"I called ahead and told them I'd be dropping by to ask a few questions," said Mitchell. "I'll make the introductions and then ask the questions you want answers to. That way you can deny you ever spoke to the young lady when the DEA comes to arrest you."

Rivera chuckled as they walked up the slate walkway, but he found the thought a bit unsettling. "Maybe you should leave out of your report that I accompanied you."

"I plan to. What exactly do you want to ask her?"

"I'm mainly interested in where she got the peyote. The name of the source. I have no interest in arresting her."

"That's good, because her father is pastor of one of our local churches. We sure don't need a big scandal in this nice little town. And besides, most people have done silly things during their youth."

"Even you, I'll bet. Care to share?"

Mitchell smiled. "I'll keep my juvenile transgressions to myself, if you don't mind."

Mitchell rang the doorbell. A tall, bald man wearing wire-rimmed glasses opened the door. He had a long face and was wearing a black shirt and black pants. He wasn't smiling.

"Come in, gentlemen," he said in a solemn tone of voice.

They entered the living room where the man's daughter and wife were waiting and sat down. The wife appeared worried, her hands tightly twisting in her lap. She was wearing a housedress and apron, and her hair was pulled straight back into a bun. The daughter, a pretty girl with long brown hair and brown eyes opened wide, was sitting erect and appeared tense and frightened. She was wearing a dress, the kind the daughter of a preacher might wear to Sunday services.

Mitchell made the introductions and began by asking the girl how she was doing.

The father answered for her. "Abigail's much better today. She had us worried for a time."

"I understand her sickness was due to the ingestion of peyote buttons. Is that correct?"

"That's what the doctor told us," said the father.

"We thank God she's going to be well," said Mrs. Nolan. "We prayed and prayed for her."

Mitchell turned to Abigail. "We need to know where you got the peyote, Abigail."

The girl looked at her father, consternation on her face.

He nodded and spoke in a soft voice. "Honey, tell the deputy where you got the peyote."

She hesitated for a long moment. "I don't want to get anyone in trouble."

"We just need to know where the stuff is coming from," said Mitchell. "Did you get it from a dealer?"

"No, I got it from one of my classmates at school."

"Which school?"

"The Utah State University branch in Moab."

"What's your classmate's name?"

She took a deep breath. "Bill Toliver. He's in my accounting class. I think he got it from a friend of his, but I'm not sure. A few of us just wanted to try some to see what it was like."

"Where does the Toliver boy live?"

"Moab."

"I don't recognize the name," said Mitchell. He glanced at Rivera who shrugged his shoulders and shook his head.

"How old is he?" asked Mitchell.

"I don't know exactly, but I'd guess he's about my age."

"Did you know Lucia Navarro?"

"Not well. She was in one of my classes at U.S.U."

"And you know what happened to her."

"Yes, Sir. I heard."

"She was experimenting with peyote and ended up dead."

A tear rolled down Abigail's cheek. "Yes, Sir."

Rivera shook his head. Abigail knew about Lucia's accident, yet she tried peyote anyway. It never ceased to amaze him what peer pressure would do to a teenager.

Mitchell stood up. "It's not smart to experiment with drugs. You never know what it's going to lead to. It could ruin your life."

She nodded, her penitent gaze on the floor.

The two deputies walked to the front door and exited, the father following them outside with a worried look on his face. "Is she going to be arrested?"

Mitchell shook his head. "I think she's learned her lesson. Just keep a close eye on her."

"I don't know what kind of person the Toliver boy is. Is there any way you can keep him from finding out that it was Abigail who identified him?"

"I understand. We'll do our best."

The two deputies walked to their vehicles. "What do you think?" asked Mitchell.

"Just teenagers having a silly adventure, I guess. But if there's a dealer in the area, we need to find out who he is and put him behind bars."

"Are you going to interview the Toliver kid?"

"I don't know. I suppose I should turn the lead over to the DEA."

Mitchell stopped walking. He looked at Rivera and smiled. "You should, but if I know you, you won't. You'll pursue it and get yourself in trouble. Lose your badge."

Rivera produced a wry expression. "You're probably right."

"It's your career, Manny. Have you thought about how you're going to explain losing your job to Gloria?"

"Good question."

"It is, isn't it? Well, follow me to Monticello and we'll pay Howard Hollingdale a visit and talk about wolves. At least you'll be working on something you're supposed to be working on."

22

THE HOLLINGDALE RESIDENCE was a sprawling one-story rock home situated on a hill overlooking the town of Monticello. To Rivera, it looked not only expensive but also ecologically designed. Rather than grass, the yard consisted of crushed gravel populated with cactus and other desert plants. There were solar panels mounted on the roof and a small wind turbine behind the house. A catchment system collected rainwater from the roof, and a white Tesla Model 3 was parked in the driveway.

The deputies approached the front door and rang the doorbell. "I hope he's here," said Mitchell. "He's an older guy who doesn't travel much anymore, so chances are excellent he's home."

They waited. Mitchell rang the doorbell a second time. Soon they heard the shuffling of feet from within and the door opened. A short man with white hair and pale skin with age spots saw Mitchell and smiled. "Hi, Emmett. I'll bet I know why you're here." He laughed a high-pitched laugh and waved them in. "I'll just bet you're going to ask me about wolves."

Mitchell introduced Rivera to Hollingdale, and the three men settled in comfortable chairs in the living room. Rivera was taken by the spectacular view through the floor-to-ceiling windows. It looked like a painting of a small town with houses, trees, and a church steeple, and beyond that, green fields and mountains.

Mitchell got right to the point. "Howard, I'm sure you've heard all the news about wolves being released in the LaSals. But did you hear about the shooting that took place up there three days ago?"

Hollingdale nodded. "I did. Damn shame. I understand the victim was a fine fellow."

Mitchell gestured toward Rivera. "Deputy Rivera of Grand County is investigating the matter and wanted to ask you a few questions."

Hollingdale shifted his gaze to Rivera. "I don't know how I can help you. I know nothing about it other than what was in the news."

Rivera didn't want to reveal his thoughts that the killer might have been an activist interested in protecting the newly released wolves from the searching eyes of a drone. He wanted to approach the subject from an oblique angle, but he had nothing credible to start with. He decided it would be best to get right to the point.

"I'd like to learn who released the wolves into the LaSals. I'm told that the release wouldn't have taken place without your knowledge and maybe even your approval."

Hollingdale stared at Rivera with an incredulous expression. After a long moment, the edges of his mouth turned slightly upward. That turned into a grin.

"Deputy…Ramirez, is it?"

"Rivera."

"Yes. Well, you *do* understand that releasing those wolves into a new habitat is not a crime, don't you? Even the federal government has done it. Surely you're aware of the wolves that were released into Yellowstone National Park under the auspices of the National Park Service. And more recently, wolves were introduced into the Western Range of the Rocky Mountains by the Colorado Parks and Wildlife people."

"I'm aware of all that, but that's not what I'm investigating."

Hollingdale leaned forward, now sitting on the edge of his chair, looking like someone eagerly awaiting the start of an intellectual duel. "Then what is it you're investigating?"

Rivera tried to remain calm and not reveal his irritation. "I'd appreciate it if you would answer the question. I just need a name. It would be most helpful."

"Assuming I know who did it—and I'm not saying I do—why should I reveal the man's identity?"

Now Rivera hoped his face wasn't flushing. "My immediate concern is not with the wolves themselves." Rivera shot a quick glance at Mitchell who seemed to be enjoying the proceedings. "I would like to meet with those who released the wolves and ask them some questions related to the shooting death of Derek Webster."

"Surely you don't believe they shot Webster."

Rivera forced a smile. "It's a simple question, and it would be most helpful if you would answer it."

Hollingdale laughed. "So your theory is the men who released the wolves into the mountains killed the drone operator to keep his drones from finding the wolves. That about it?"

"Just answer the question, please."

"I don't have to answer any of your questions, Deputy Whatever-Your-Name-Is. You do understand that, don't you? If not, I can call my attorney. I'm sure he would be most happy to come over here and explain it to you. Besides, you're outside of your jurisdiction." He smiled and tilted his chin upward in a kind of challenging manner.

"Well, I guess I'm wasting my time. I believe I'm done here." Rivera stood up.

"Well now, hold on just a minute." Hollingdale laughed an artificial laugh, then spoke in a patronizing tone of voice. "You shouldn't give up so easily, Deputy. Maybe there's a way I can help you without getting my friends in trouble. It's true that I know the men who released the wolves. The guy in charge of the operation is a friend of mine. I call him Whitey, but of course, Whitey's not his real name—that shall remain a secret. But I believe I can tell you something useful."

"All right." He sat down.

"Perhaps you don't appreciate the extent to which we environmentalists are able to gather intelligence about what the other side is thinking and doing. We knew that the ranchers formed a coalition after the notice about the wolf release appeared in the newspaper. And we knew about Eddie Zander as soon as they hired him. We've run across him before. He's good at what he does. But word spreads fast among concerned environmentalists. My point is that there are plenty of environmentalists that knew the wolves were in danger. Most are law abiding citizens that want a better world. Others are less reasonable and will do almost anything to advance their cause. So it's possible one of the latter types got wind of Derek and the work he was hired to do for Eddie. How might they have done that? Any number of ways. They could have bugged Eddie's motel room, for example. I know they keep a close eye on him wherever he goes. So it's therefore possible that one of them killed Derek to prevent his drones from locating the wolves. But it wasn't Whitey."

"How do you know that?"

"On the day of the shooting in the LaSals, I received a telephone call from him. I recognized the Caller ID number because I've seen it a couple of dozen times. He was calling from the landline phone at his house in McCall, Idaho, so he couldn't have been the shooter. Nor could he have seen anything useful to your investigation. He was over five-hundred miles away."

"Thank you. That's helpful. But I would still like to talk with him."

"As I said, I won't give you his name, but I *can* tell you he plans to make a similar release into the Abajo Mountains, which I greatly favor. Why should I tell you something that might inhibit him from doing so?"

After a few more unsuccessful attempts at getting a name, the two deputies left the house and headed for their vehicles.

"You handled that well," said a grinning Mitchell.

"That wasn't very pleasant. He's an irritating fellow."

Mitchell chuckled. "Don't say I didn't warn you."

"Why does he act like that?"

"I don't know. But don't feel bad. He does that to everyone he meets for the first time. He did the same thing to me when I was introduced to him years ago."

"Seems unnecessary."

"I think when he meets someone for the first time, he has a need to establish the pecking order. Him on top, everyone else below him."

"Has he got any friends?"

Mitchell thought. "None I know of, but everyone in the environmental activist community holds him in high esteem."

"Unusual fellow."

Rivera said goodbye to his friend and headed back to Moab.

23

RIVERA WAS MILDLY convinced that Hollingdale was telling the truth, but he couldn't be certain. He still wanted to talk with Whitey himself. The deputy tried to picture how the wolf release had taken place. Each wolf must have been housed in a separate cage. And the cages had to be large to contain a wolf. Six cages would require a lot of space. And there had to be at least two humans to handle the cages. The humans had to have steel shields or some other type of protection so a wolf couldn't easily turn on them when it was released. The vehicle therefore had to be large, perhaps an oversized van or a large truck. There were probably three drop-offs, one for each mated pair, each pair in a different location in the mountains.

His thoughts went back to the notice in the newspaper announcing that wolves now roamed in the LaSals. It may have been timed to appear a day or two after they were released. At that point, the individuals involved were free to leave Moab, their mission having been completed. As he thought about the timeline of events, he realized that they'd probably left Moab before Derek was killed. That's what Hollingdale had stated. But he wanted to be sure. He wanted to talk with Whitey himself.

Maybe someone at the newspaper remembered who had placed the notice. Perhaps they'd paid for it by writing a check that he could trace through the newspaper's bank. He shook his head, realizing that was probably wishful thinking brought about by his lack of progress thus far.

Nevertheless, when he got back into town, he stopped at the newspaper office to see what he could learn. Liddie was on duty at the front counter. In her late twenties, she was tall with long, stringy blonde hair. Rivera had known her since she began working at the newspaper ten years ago.

"Hi, Manny. I hope you're here to place another ad." She giggled and brushed a strand of hair out of her eye and tucked it over her ear. "That last one you placed was a big hit. We sold out in a few hours and had to print a second edition."

"No more ads for me, Liddie. I believe one was my limit."

"Oh, shucks. I was hoping for some excitement around here."

"I came in to see if anyone remembered who placed that notice in the paper about releasing wolves into the LaSals."

"Oh, I remember him." She smiled and batted her eyelashes. "He was a real hunk. I remember he was in a big hurry. He dropped off the ad copy and paid in cash."

"What did he look like?"

"About five-feet-ten inches tall, dreamy blue eyes, and shoulder length hair that was blond, almost white. He had a face like a movie star. I asked him how long he'd be in town, thinking maybe we could meet for a drink. But he was in a big hurry and left before I could get him interested."

"Do you remember his name?"

"He never told me his name."

"How about his age?"

"I'd say mid-thirties."

"Anything else you can remember about him?"

She thought for a moment. "I noticed he had a wolf's head tattoo on his forearm. That's about it. I glanced out the front window and watched him as he walked away." She grinned. "He had a real cute butt. He got into the driver's side of one of those oversized panel trucks. It was white. I noticed it had Idaho plates. There was another guy sitting in the passenger seat, but I didn't get a good look at him. The truck pulled away and, sadly, I never saw my dreamboat again."

Rivera thought about the planned wolf release in the Abajos that Howard Hollingdale mentioned. It was possible Whitey would return. "Liddie, he might come back. If you see him again, will you write down his license number and give me a call?"

She grinned. "Sure, Manny. Now you've got my hopes up."

Rivera returned to his pickup and sat there thinking. It was pretty certain that Whitey had left Moab before Derek was killed and would therefore be unable to supply Rivera with useful information. He was beginning to get the feeling that he'd reached a dead end in his investigation. Nothing seemed to be jelling. He decided to go back to the impound lot and take a fresh look at the video from the day of the shooting.

Two hours later, after viewing the video from beginning to end, he had come up with two more tidbits of information worthy of follow-up. The first was the license plate of the vehicle that Gene Squires's girlfriend had parked at the Miner's Basin trailhead. Derek's drone had swooped down close enough so that Rivera was able to zoom in on the license number and read it. The second item worthy of follow-up was the archeological dig taking place in the side canyon that the drone's camera had captured. Perhaps someone at the site had seen something.

He returned to his office and called Ralph Lansing at the BLM Field Office. He explained the situation to Lansing, gave him his best estimate of the GPS coordinates of the dig, and learned that the location was on National Forest land, not BLM land. It was under the jurisdiction of the U.S. Department of Agriculture, not the Department of the Interior. There were different procedures and regulations in each department. Lansing began explaining the differences.

As Lansing droned on, Rivera felt a rising level of irritation. Why have two different sets of procedures? Only the federal government would operate in such a wasteful manner. Up in the LaSals, there are imaginary boundaries between BLM land and National Forest land. Why, when one steps across one of these imaginary lines, do the rules and procedures change? Two sets of regulations and two separate organizations to manage them. Rivera shook his head. It would be funny if it wasn't so annoying.

Lansing finally finished his explanation.

"Can you tell me who to call at the National Forest Service?" Rivera tried to keep the frustration out of his voice.

"I know the guy. I'll call him and get right back to you."

"Thanks, Ralph." Rivera felt relieved. While he waited, he checked the Utah Department of Motor Vehicles database and learned the identity of the owner of the vehicle parked at the Miner's Basin trailhead. Her name was Elizabeth Blackstone and she lived in the small town of Green River on the western margin of Grand County. Rather than call her, Rivera decided he would drive out there and talk to her face-to-face.

Ten minutes later, Rivera's telephone rang. It was Lansing.

"Okay, Manny, it's a legitimate dig. A Fieldwork Authorization was issued by the National Forest Service to Professor Edmund Van Nostrand four months ago. He's an anthropologist from the University of Colorado in Boulder. He's working the dig with a couple of his students." Lansing recited the professor's cell phone number which Rivera jotted into his notepad.

"Great. Thanks, Ralph."

Rivera called the professor. Luckily, he was not at the dig, deep in a canyon where the cell phone signals might not penetrate. He was in Moab at City Market picking up groceries and supplies. Rivera arranged to meet him in the City Market parking lot.

He had expected Professor Van Nostrand to be an older man with a gray beard, but it turned out he looked to be about Rivera's age. He was well-tanned and wore jeans, a blue work shirt, and boots.

After the preliminaries, Rivera told him he was investigating the shooting of Derek Webster. He took him back to the day in question, verified that the professor was there that day, and asked him if he had seen anyone else in the canyon besides his two student helpers.

Van Nostrand thought for a long moment. "You know, we've been out there for a couple of months, digging, sorting, and cataloguing. We may be onto an important discovery related to the timing of the Anasazi departure.

So we were pretty well focused on our work. All the days seem to run together, but I'm pretty sure I remember the day in question. That's the day one of my students uncovered a perfect obsidian spearpoint. And yes, I did see a couple of hunters that day."

"Where were they when you saw them?"

"They were hiking up the main canyon. We were about a hundred yards away working in a side canyon. I saw one, then about fifteen minutes later, I saw a second one."

"Can you describe them?"

"I'm afraid not. I have good eyesight, but they were too far away. They both looked like men. I do remember that one was wearing orange, and the other was dressed in more of a greenish brown jacket. The one wearing orange was wearing an orange baseball cap, and the other one was wearing a wide-brimmed hat. That's all I remember. Oh, wait. I also remember that the guy with the wide-brimmed hat was using some sort of hiking stick or pole."

"Which one was wearing orange, the first to pass or the second?"

"The second."

Van Nostrand's observations were consistent with what Rivera had observed on the video recording taken on the day of the shooting. "Did you hear any gunshots?"

"You know, we hear them almost every day out there—it's hunting season. But that day, we heard one that was closer than usual. I remember that one of my students remarked about it. He wondered if we were safe. I figured one of the hunters I saw took a shot at an animal."

"Was that before or after you saw the two hunters?"

"After. I'd say about twenty minutes after."

Rivera thanked the professor for his help, got into his vehicle, and headed north out of town. As he drove, he wondered if the hiker in the greenish brown jacket might have been the shooter. If he'd been a hunter, he might have been wearing orange. But some hunters wear camouflage outfits to stay hidden from their prey. And from a distance, camo clothing might appear greenish brown.

24

AFTER CLEARING HIS visit to Emery County with the local sheriff, Rivera drove north to Interstate-70 and turned west, headed for the town of Green River to question Elizabeth Blackstone about her boyfriend Gene Squires. As he drove, his thoughts drifted back to the senseless death of Lucia Navarro after she had experimented with peyote. He wanted to confront Bill Toliver, the young man who Abigail Nolan had identified as the source of the peyote and grill him on how he had obtained it. He also wanted to know if there was a pusher operating in the area. He felt a responsibility to the community and to Mr. Navarro to find out. Rivera knew full well that he shouldn't be involving himself in the case, but he felt a strong drive to do so. Maybe he was also driven by his low regard for Bill Masters, his DEA nemesis, and wouldn't mind solving Masters's case before he was able to. But he liked his boss and didn't want to get her in trouble with the feds. It was a dilemma, and he began wondering if there was a solution.

Fifteen miles later, the answer came to him. His friend Chris Carey was always eager to help Rivera with his cases as it helped satisfy his need to continue functioning as an investigative journalist. Rivera decided he would ask Chris to visit Bill Toliver and see if he could find out where the young man had gotten the peyote. Carey wouldn't be breaking any laws in the process. If Toliver was willing to give an honest answer, Rivera would be one step closer to finding out who the ultimate dealer was and one step closer to giving Lucia's father a satisfactory answer to his question.

He called Carey and presented him with the idea. Carey jumped at the opportunity and said he would get right on it. It turned out that Carey knew the Toliver family well and had been friends with Toliver's grandfather for decades. Ah, the benefits of living in a small town, thought Rivera.

Rivera parked at the curb in front of Elizabeth Blackstone's house. It was a one-story structure with white clapboard siding and yellow trim. The front yard was mostly dirt with a smattering of local bushes and weeds, and there was a well-tended melon garden flourishing on the side of the house.

A woman in her twenties with long blonde hair was sitting on the front porch reading a book and smoking a cigarette. She was wearing khaki shorts and a pink tank top. A small black and white dog was curled up at her feet.

As Rivera approached, she studied him and produced a smile. "Hi. If you're looking for my grandparents, they're at the Senior Center."

"Are you Elizabeth Blackstone?"

Her smile wavered. "Yes, I am. Everyone calls me Liz."

Rivera introduced himself. "I'd like to ask you some questions about Gene Squires."

The smile disappeared. "What kind of questions?"

When he started to climb the steps to the porch, the dog ran to the top of the stairs and stood there, growling, baring its teeth, and barking. Rivera took a step backwards.

"Pluto, stop!" She looked irritated and raised her voice. "Pluto, stop!"

The barking continued. "Okay Mister, time for you to go in the house." She put her cigarette in an ashtray, picked up the dog, and deposited him inside the house. Rivera could still hear the barking coming from inside.

"Now what's this about Gene Squires?"

Rivera ascended the steps. "I'd like to learn more about him and his activities. It's part of an investigation I'm conducting."

She frowned and took a drag on her cigarette. "Well, go ahead and ask your questions. I can't guarantee I'll answer them."

"What's your relationship with Squires?"

She laughed, emitting a burst of smoke from her mouth and nose. "I'm guessing you already know the answer to that. That's why you're here."

"I'd like to hear *your* answer."

"All right. We used to date."

"Used to?" Rivera appreciated her forthrightness. He was glad not to have another interview like the one he had with Howard Hollingdale.

"That's right, used to. It's over. It was fun until it got complicated."

"Complicated how?"

"He told me he was being blackmailed. I didn't need that kind of drama in my life. I like to keep things simple. Simple, simple, simple. It's easier to enjoy life that way."

"So you broke it off."

"Damn right."

"When was that?"

"Yesterday."

"Did he say how long the blackmailing had been going on?"

"Yeah. He said several weeks."

"Was the blackmailing the only reason you broke off the relationship?"

"Well, that was the main reason, but the relationship was also getting kind of stale, if you know what I mean. He's a handsome man, but he seemed to lack character or drive." She shrugged. "He's boring."

"Did he mention how he was being blackmailed?"

"It was what you'd expect. Pay up or his little affair with Liz would be made public. He was scared to death. Personally, I didn't care, one way or the other. Humans make too big a deal out of sex. Look at the animals. They handle all that mating business in a matter-of-fact way. Oh, they might fight to see who mates with whom, but they don't have all the social and moral hangups we humans have."

"Did he say who was blackmailing him?"

"He said he didn't know. It was just a voice on the other end of the telephone line."

"So when you found out about the blackmail, you broke off the relationship."

"Right. And that's everything I know about it. Now, I'd appreciate it if you would leave before my grandparents return. I don't want to have to explain to them why I'm being interviewed by a deputy."

Rivera had no more questions. "I understand. If I need to talk again, I'll call you instead of visiting." He pulled his notepad from his shirt pocket. "What's your cell phone number?"

She recited it for him, and he jotted it down.

"I may need to talk with Gene Squires too. Do you have his cell phone number?"

She told him.

Rivera drove off, wondering what in the world blackmailing Gene Squires might have to do with the

175

murder of Derek Webster. Maybe nothing, but it was not like him to ignore such possibilities.

25

DRIVING BACK TO Moab, Rivera reflected on the progress of his investigation. It wasn't impressive. Two of the three possible scenarios related to Derek's drone business had crumbled. The diggings in the ghost town on Lucas Nichols's ranch were the work of kids at play. And it appeared that the group which released the wolves into the LaSals most likely were back in Idaho on the day Derek was shot.

And now, the last scenario Rivera had postulated was seriously in doubt. It no longer seemed probable that Gene Squires had noticed the drone tracking his movements and set out to kill the drone operator in order to keep his trysts with Liz Blackstone secret. From the descriptions of Squires by his wife and his girlfriend, he didn't seem the type that would engage in violence. But Rivera needed to be sure. He decided to meet with Squires himself and size him up.

At the office, he called Squires on his cell phone, introduced himself, and told him he'd like to meet with him and ask him a few questions. Rivera said he was aware of the blackmailing that was going on and wanted to learn more about it. He explained that the information might be helpful in another case he was investigating. Squires seemed confused, and Rivera found it necessary to repeat his request several times. Squires finally acceded, but only on the condition that they meet in private. He didn't want anyone to learn about the meeting and start asking him a lot of questions. Rivera saw no harm in accommodating him. They decided to meet in a remote location, where hopefully no one would recognize Squires.

Rivera drove home, parked at his house, and drove his personal pickup truck to the Sand Flats Recreation Area a couple of miles east of town. He parked at the far end of the parking lot, away from other vehicles, and waited. Ten minutes later, a purple Jeep pulled into the lot. The driver paused for a moment and scanned the parking area, then slowly drove over and stopped next to Rivera's vehicle so that the driver's side windows were facing each other. When the man lowered his window, Rivera saw a handsome but frightened fellow staring at him with wide-open eyes. His face matched the photograph Rivera had seen in Ginny Hempstead's living room.

"Deputy Rivera?"

"Yes. And you're Gene Squires?"

"Yes, I am."

"Thanks for meeting with me. I need to ask you some questions about this blackmail business you're being subjected to." Rivera was careful with his words.

He didn't want to reveal that Squires's wife had hired a private investigator to document the husband's infidelity.

"How did you know I was being blackmailed?"

"How about I ask the questions and you provide the answers. That's the way this is supposed to work. And that's the way we might be able to identify the blackmailer and shut him down."

"Oh. Well, sure. I was just curious." Squires's gaze flitted around the parking lot as he spoke. "To tell you the truth, I'm very worried."

"Tell me about the blackmail."

"If I do, I'll also be revealing something I want kept secret."

"You're talking about your extramarital affair with that blonde?"

Squires's jaw dropped. "You know about that?"

"It's not general knowledge. I ran across the information because of an unrelated crime I'm investigating."

"Are you sure it's not general knowledge?"

"As sure as I can be. Now, what about the blackmail? How did it work?"

Squires inhaled a deep breath and let it out. "I got a call on my cell phone about a month ago. The caller said he knew about the affair, and if I wanted it kept secret, I had to pay him a thousand dollars a week in cash. I agreed. Money's not a problem for me. So that's what I've been doing. I can't afford to have my wife find out."

"How do you deliver the money to the blackmailer?"

"He calls me every Saturday at exactly noon on that public telephone outside the Moab Information Center. I get there five minutes early and wait. When the phone rings, I answer it right away. He tells me where to leave the cash and instructs me to put it there within the hour. It's a different place each time. Typically somewhere easily accessible in the LaSals."

"Where did you leave it last time?"

"Under a rock alongside the Castleton Gateway Road where it intersects with the LaSal Loop Road."

"Well, tomorrow is Saturday, so you'll be getting another call. Meet with me here at ten in the morning so I can record the serial numbers of the bills. After he calls you at noon, follow his instructions to the letter, but call me from your cell phone and let me know where you are headed. I'll arrange to have a surprise party waiting for whoever comes to pick up the cash."

Squires hesitated. His gaze shifted from Rivera to the ground and back to Rivera. "I've got a bad feeling about this. I'm worried my wife will find out and I'll lose her. I need to think this through. Can I call you this evening and let you know about tomorrow?"

"Sure." Rivera gave him a card containing his cell phone number. "But I have one request. Even if you decide not to help me, at least write down the serial numbers of the bills and save the list. It might come in handy later."

"Okay. I guess I can do that." Squires had a defeated look on his face. "Can I leave now?"

"Sure. We're finished here."

Squires raised his window and slowly drove off.

As the deputy exited the parking lot, he reflected on Squires. He was a pathetic excuse for a man, and Ginny Hempstead deserved better. But that was none of his business. Having now met Squires, Rivera was convinced that the man could neither plan a murder nor execute one. Someone else must have killed Derek Webster. But who? And why? Maybe the motive was of a personal nature and not related to his drone business. Or maybe the shooting was a hunting accident, and Rivera had misjudged the entire situation.

He felt like he was back at square one in his investigation. He was beginning to feel pangs of self-doubt. Might this case be his first failure? He dwelled on that question for a while, then remembered having these same feelings at some juncture in each one of his previous cases. It was natural. A fear of failure. He forced himself to relax and resumed analyzing the facts of the case.

Nearly all the information he had gathered thus far had come from the videos Derek recorded. Perhaps there was more in those videos, something important that Rivera had overlooked. He'd reviewed the contents of the video stored in Derek's vehicle a second time and learned a few additional tidbits of information by doing so. Perhaps he should do the same thing with the videos in the storage unit. In his haste to view them, he might have missed something.

Rivera drove home, swapped vehicles, and drove to Derek's storage unit. He sat down in front of the computer, accessed the list of files, skipped down to those related to Webster Drone Services, and began stepping through each video. It was then he remembered he'd skipped over most of the Phil Broderick entries, having assumed they all showed pretty much the same thing—a man and a woman hiking into the woods until they disappeared under the forest canopy. This time, he decided to check each video, skipping nothing, and playing them in their entirety. It would be time-consuming, but at this point he didn't have a better idea.

He started with *Broderick001,* the first paid assignment in Derek's journal, and the first of many assignments from Phil Broderick. He played the video from beginning to end. It was just as he remembered it and he saw nothing particularly noteworthy. Just Gene Squires waiting for Elizabeth Blackstone, her arrival, their embraces and kisses, and their walk into the woods, then disappearing under the tree canopy. *Broderick002,* the second Phil Broderick entry, showed pretty much the same thing.

It was in *Broderick003* that he saw something entirely different. This time, the couple entered the woods, disappeared under the forest canopy, and reappeared on the other side in an open field of tall golden grasses.

There, they spread a blanket on the ground and, apparently assuming the tall grass would shield them from the view of anyone in the area, undressed, and engaged in the lovemaking that Ginny Hempstead had wanted documented. He checked the date of the video. It was three weeks old. Then he checked the subsequent Phil Broderick entries and saw more of the same. So why hadn't Broderick reported this information to Ginny? Was it because he wanted the weekly retainer fees to keep coming in? Was he perpetrating a fraud at Ginny's expense?

It occurred to him that Broderick might also be the blackmailer. A larger picture of deceit was emerging in Rivera's mind. Broderick could be playing both ends against the middle by collecting weekly retainer fees from Ginny while not informing her that he already had the goods on her husband, and also collecting blackmail money each week from her husband in exchange for the private investigator's silence. Two separate sources of income, two separate crimes. Clever, thought Rivera, but it was only conjecture. He needed proof.

Taking that logic a step further, it raised a more sinister question. Was it possible that Phil Broderick had killed Derek Webster? Derek must have realized that the goal of the assignment had been achieved and that the private investigator was simply bilking the client for more money. He was the only person who could expose Broderick's fraud.

Rivera locked up the storage unit. He had a lot of thinking to do about Broderick and his activities. He wanted to analyze all the possibilities before he started making accusations. On the way back to the office, his cell phone buzzed. The caller was Chris Carey.

"Manny, I met with the young man we talked about. Why don't you stop by the house when you get a chance and I'll fill you in."

Rivera was busy and in a hurry, but his strong desire to help Emiliano Navarro motivated him to take a break. "How about right now?"

"Sure. I'll brew us some coffee."

Rivera liked Carey's tone of voice. It was enthusiastic and sounded like he had learned something useful from Bill Toliver about the source of peyote in Grand County. Rivera was eager to hear what his friend had learned.

26

CAREY'S FRONT DOOR opened, and the journalist stood there with a big grin on his face. He waved Rivera inside. "C'mon in. Coffee's about ready. Why don't you go into the den and get comfortable while I pour us a couple of mugs. I've got some really good stuff for you."

Rivera sat on a padded leather chair, eager to learn what Carey had to say. He looked around the room while he waited. He'd been here many times seeking Carey's advice or asking him for assistance. It was a familiar setting. There were shelves crammed with books, piles of yellowing newspapers on a table, file cabinets full of old clippings, and an Underwood typewriter with round black keys and white letters that Carey had used over fifty years ago as a cub reporter working at his first newspaper job. On one wall was a framed photograph of Carey standing with a former Utah governor. Other photographs showed him with a Utah senator, several congressmen, and other noteworthy figures including Mickey Mantle, Angie Dickenson, Dean Martin, and Buddy Holly. On an adjacent wall were framed certificates of achievement and appreciation which had been presented to Carey over the years. It was a perfect setting for someone who had devoted his life to newspaper journalism. The room even smelled like newsprint. For some reason, Rivera always felt a reassuring comfort here. Maybe because, in a way, it represented a bastion of truth.

Carey returned and handed him a mug of coffee, then clinked his own mug against Rivera's. "Here's to a successful conspiracy. Thanks for including me." He sat behind a walnut desk cluttered with newspapers and magazines.

"You've been a great help on a lot of my cases. We should probably make you an honorary deputy." Rivera took a couple of sips. "Great coffee, thanks."

"I've known the Toliver family for thirty years," Carey began. "Bill's grandfather and I have been close friends all that time. And I've known Bill since the day he was born. I'm kind of like an uncle to him. He sometimes comes here to ask me questions about life, careers, family, and a lot of those things an eighteen-year-old wonders about. He's a good kid and a basketball nut, always on the municipal courts wearing a ball cap backwards and shooting hoops. He's played in the Moab intramural league since he was twelve. So I drove to the courts first, and there he was, practicing three-point shots by himself. First thing I noticed was that he had a split lip and a black eye. I asked him what happened. He laughed and said intramural basketball in Moab was very competitive and sometimes things get rough under the basket. He said it's happened to him before, and it'll probably happen again. So much for friendly competition.

"I said I hoped he had time to sit and talk for a while because I wanted to ask him a few questions of a personal nature. He said sure. We sat down on a bench, and I asked him if he'd ever experimented with drugs. I know him well enough to be blunt like that. He smiled and stared at me for a moment. Then he asked me if I was planning to write an article about drug use. I said maybe, I wasn't sure yet. I told him I was in the data gathering stage. It was a dishonest answer intended to evade the question, and I hope he'll forgive me if he ever finds out. He shrugged and said he'd tried marijuana a few times but none of the heavy stuff like cocaine or heroin.

"I asked him if he'd ever tried peyote. He said yes, a couple of times. He and a group of fellow U.S.U. students met in the LaSals one night and tried it, just for fun. One guy in the group had gotten ahold of some. Bill said he didn't know where the guy got it. They had all heard about the hallucinations peyote induced and wanted to try it just to see what would happen. He said that was the night Lucia Navarro had died in the automobile accident. He felt horrible about what had happened to her. She was a fine girl. And smart. Bill and a few other students used to go to her house a couple of times a month to play cards and board games. He said that after her accident, he swore he'd never try peyote again. But he'd tried it a second time anyway with some of those same students. He said it was always fun being with them. They met in the mountains after dark, started a bonfire, and chewed on the peyote buttons. He said it produced some really weird psychedelic images. He had difficulty describing them. He talked about an increased sense of connection with the universe, a feeling of euphoria, an altered perception of colors and sounds, and talking plants. Things like that. I'm not sure he really understood what he was saying. I certainly didn't.

"I asked him if he planned to try peyote again. He said no, because after it was over, he felt nauseous all the next day. I was relieved to hear that. Then I asked him who it was that provided the peyote to the group. He laughed and said it was a drop-out from the college who fancied himself as a Native American. He was an Anglo but liked to pretend he was Navajo. He let his hair grow real long, all the way down his back. Bill said he thought the guy dyed his hair to make it look darker. He usually wore a red headband. Sometimes his hair was done up in a bun, sometimes in long braids. Bill called him an Indian wannabe. When they got together to try the peyote, he painted his cheeks with red and black stripes and referred to himself as the Peyote Chief.

"I asked him the name of the Peyote Chief and said I'd like to interview him too." Here, Carey paused for dramatic effect and smiled, having reached the pinnacle of his story. "Bill said the guy's name is Jimmy Ventner. He used to be in some of Bill's classes, but he dropped out of school the previous semester. He's a few years older than the other students. Bill said Ventner was visiting relatives in Denver now and wouldn't be back home until very late Saturday night. And that's pretty much the story. Does that help?"

"It helps quite a lot, Chris. Thank you. That puts us one step closer to the source. I wonder if Ventner has a supplier on the Navajo Reservation."

"Could be. Anything else I can do? Maybe interview the Peyote Chief for you?"

"Better not. We might be getting close to the prime source, and I don't want to see you get in trouble with some ruthless drug pusher. Do you know Ventner's address?"

"Bill said he lives out in Cisco at his brother's place. He sketched out a map for me." Carey pulled a hand drawn map from his shirt pocket and handed it to Rivera.

"I'll plan to visit him Sunday morning. That'll give me plenty of time to think about how to proceed." From here on, there was no telling what dangers lie ahead, not just with the dealer, but also with the DEA. He thanked Carey again and returned to his office.

27

RIVERA RETRIEVED A MUG of coffee from the break room, all the while thinking he should cut down on his coffee consumption. He shrugged off that idea and smiled, deciding today wasn't the best time. Maybe tomorrow would be better. It was the same decision process he went through almost every day.

He closed his office door to keep out the noise and discourage interruptions, sat in his chair, and took a couple of sips. He had a lot of thinking to do about the Derek Webster murder. At first glance, it appeared that Phil Broderick was the only sensible culprit. Rivera thought it all through again. Broderick could continue receiving weekly payments from both Ginny Hempstead and Gene Squires for a long time, as long as the investigation he was conducting remained unsolved. After Derek gave him the incriminating video on a thumb drive, it was then that Broderick might have seen Derek as a threat to his scheme. Derek would know that the job had been completed, yet Broderick kept the surveillance project active. And that might be a motive for murder. Rivera thought through that scenario, testing it for assumptions. There was one. It assumed that Derek gave the video in question to Broderick. If that were the case, he would have given it to him stored on a thumb drive. Was there any way to establish that the file had been written to a thumb drive? Possibly. Maybe there was some kind of record of the transfer stored in the computer. Now Rivera needed Charlie Savage's help again. He gave him a call.

"Hi, Manny. How can I help you?"

"Charlie, is there any way to determine if a specific file in Derek's computer has been written to a thumb drive?"

"Indeed there is, my good man. Rather than have me explain it over the phone, how about meeting me at Derek's storage unit in five minutes. I'll check that out for you."

"Great. Thanks, Charlie."

Rivera unlocked the door of the storage unit and the two men entered. Savage turned the system on and displayed the list of files associated with Derek's drone business.

"Which file are you interested in?"

Rivera pointed to the *Broderick003* file.

Savage hit a few keystrokes and peered at the monitor. "Yep. It was definitely transferred to a thumb drive. He read off the date of the transfer to Rivera. "It was transferred the same day it was recorded by the drone's camera. About four hours later. Anything else?"

In Rivera's mind, that cinched it. There was no reason for Derek to write the file to a thumb drive unless he planned to give it to Broderick. So Rivera figured his hypothesis had to be correct. Broderick had incriminating evidence of Gene Squires's affair for the last several weeks without informing his client Ginny Hempstead, and he'd been collecting fees from her all along. Rivera felt certain Broderick would be the one to pick up Squires's cash on Saturday.

Were there other possibilities? After some thought, Rivera identified one. It was conceivable that Broderick was perpetrating a fraud on Ginny Hempstead but was not the blackmailer. In that event, Derek himself might have been the blackmailer. As Rivera dwelled on that thought, another possibility occurred to him. Elizabeth Blackstone, by herself or with a cohort, could have been the blackmailer. Rivera scratched his head and continued that line of thought.

So was the culprit Broderick, Derek, Liz, or someone else? He couldn't be certain. No problem. Tomorrow the question would answer itself. Whoever showed up to pick up the blackmail money was the guilty party. He suspected it would be Broderick, and that the private investigator was guilty not only of fraud and blackmail, but also murder.

Rivera looked at his watch. He was supposed to be keeping the sheriff updated on his progress. He returned to the office and knocked on her open door.

"What's up on the Derek Webster case?"

He briefed her on the details of his investigation and the progress he was making, which, as he listened to his own words, didn't sound like much. It sounded like he was lost in possibilities.

"So what's your next step?"

He told her about his plan to follow the money tomorrow morning.

"Okay. Let me know when it's done and who the mystery blackmailer is."

Rivera stood up. "Any news from our DEA friends on the peyote investigation?"

She smiled. "Not a word. I'm pretty sure keeping Manny Rivera up to date on their progress is not at the top of their to-do list."

"I know. If they ever break the case, I'll probably have to learn about it from the newspapers."

That evening at home, Rivera received a call on his cell phone. It was Gene Squires stating he had no interest in cooperating with Rivera on trapping the blackmailer. He'd rather pay the money than risk having Ginny find out about his affair. No matter, tomorrow morning Rivera would tail Squires from the phone booth at the Moab Information Center to the drop off point for the money. Then he would wait nearby hidden in some inconspicuous spot and arrest whoever came to pick it up.

28

IT WAS MORNING, and Rivera was eager to get started. He fixed breakfast for himself at home and killed time in the office updating and polishing his report. He looked at his watch a couple of dozen times while he waited. Finally it was 11:24 a.m., about time to get in position to follow Gene Squires and the blackmail money to the drop-off point.

He drove to Pasta Jay's Restaurant in his personal vehicle and sat at an inside table adjacent to a window. He ordered a salad, and watched tourists come and go in the parking lot of the Moab Information Center across the street. He paid the check in advance so that he could depart at a moment's notice. Around 11:48 a.m., Squires pulled into the Moab Information Center parking lot in his purple Jeep and parked. He positioned himself at the public telephone mounted on the outside wall of the building. Squires waited, checking his watch every minute or two.

At exactly noon, Rivera watched Squires reach for the phone and pick it up. The conversation lasted two minutes with Squires jotting down notes on a folded sheet of paper. He hung up the phone, hurried to his purple Jeep, and headed north out of town. Rivera followed him at a safe distance, hoping Squires wouldn't recognize the deputy's personal vehicle from their earlier meeting. He called the dispatcher and updated her on his location and plans.

Squires turned onto Hwy 128 and proceeded upriver. Twenty miles later, he turned right on Onion Creek Road, an unpaved road that led into the foothills of the LaSal Mountains. The road crisscrossed Onion Creek several times as it gained altitude. Just past the fourth creek crossing, Squires stopped, got out of his Jeep, and stood there for a long moment. He was looking down and seemed to be studying the side of the road. Rivera stopped about a hundred and fifty yards behind him where an overgrown two track joined the gravel road from the right. He watched Squires through his binoculars. Squires reached into his shirt pocket, extracted what appeared to be a white envelope, and placed it under a large rock on the left side of the road.

When Rivera saw Squires get back into his Jeep, he turned onto the two track and drove through the sage and black brush until the road curved behind a red rock hillside and he was out of sight. There he stopped and again updated the dispatcher. He got out of his vehicle, strapped on his handgun, and grabbed his badge and binoculars. He climbed to the top of the hill and hid behind a cliffrose bush, looking down at the gravel road. Despite the lateness of the season, there were still some yellow blossoms on the bush, and a few bumblebees were buzzing about, trying to extract the last few morsels of nectar. Soon, Squires's Jeep passed by, heading back toward Hwy 128. In a few minutes, it was out of sight. Now Rivera descended from the hill and moved closer to the drop-off point. He hid in a thicket of bushes about forty yards from the rock. His plan was to sit and wait. He kept an eye on the rock and periodically updated the dispatcher in a low voice. He hoped the blackmailer would arrive soon.

After an hour of waiting, Rivera began wondering if he'd made a miscalculation. He'd figured that the money would be picked up shortly after Squires left. The Onion Creek Road was rarely used, with only a few vehicles passing through each day. Perhaps the blackmailer was being ultra cautious. He might even wait until dark. Now Rivera wished he'd brought along something to read.

As he lay there, his nostrils picked up the faint scent of something unpleasant, yet vaguely familiar. It smelled like rotten eggs. Hydrogen sulfide, he realized. It brought back memories of his first murder case. He was a rookie deputy with no investigative experience when he was assigned a high-profile murder case by his then-boss Sheriff Leroy Bradshaw. He smiled when he remembered how nervous he'd been at the assignment. His investigation was helped by an encounter with four young people on a letterboxing journey. They were following a trail of hidden letterboxes across the backcountry, each box containing directions for finding the next. Rivera had never heard of letterboxing before meeting them, and learning about it enabled him to discover a letterbox just off the Onion Creek Road which turned out to be a key in his breaking the case. It was near a spring that emitted water and traces of hydrogen sulfide. He'd smelled that same unpleasant hydrogen sulfide odor during his search for the letterbox. He believed it was that odor that gave Onion Creek its name.

A dozen years had passed since then, and Rivera, at this point in his career, had many murder investigations under his belt. He loved his job and had been successful in breaking each of his previous cases. He hoped this one would be no different.

29

THE APPEARANCE OF a dust plume on the lower part of Onion Creek Road caught Rivera's eye. Hopefully, he thought, someone was coming to retrieve the cash. He waited and watched. Soon he could see that the source of the dust was a white pickup truck. It disappeared behind the undulations in the terrain and reappeared again several times as it neared Rivera's position. He crouched low in the bushes, eyes locked onto the slow-moving pickup as it drew closer. Soon, through the windshield, he could see that the driver was Phil Broderick, just as he had expected.

Broderick parked next to the rock, got out of his vehicle, and surveyed the area, making sure he was alone. He walked a few steps toward the rock and stood there, stretching out his back and glancing around at his surroundings. Then he quickly reached down and flipped the rock over. He picked up the envelope and looked inside. Rivera could see a smile appear on Broderick's face.

Rivera moved out of the bushes toward the road and drew his weapon, as it wouldn't be unusual for a private investigator to be carrying a handgun. He quietly approached Broderick, using Broderick's truck to shield him from view. Broderick was busy counting the money.

Rivera snuck up behind him, keeping his eyes locked on the private investigator. He saw Broderick stuff the cash into his pants pocket, then crumple up the envelope and toss it onto the front seat of his vehicle.

"Freeze, Broderick," said Rivera.

Broderick's head jerked up. He looked at Rivera with a surprised look on his face.

"You're under arrest."

Broderick looked angry. "What the hell for? I ain't doing nothing wrong."

"Turn around and put your hands behind your back."

Broderick complied as ordered. "What's going on? I just came out here for a drive in the country. See the sights and get some fresh air."

Rivera cuffed him, patted him down, and read him his rights. He was unarmed.

"You picked up an envelope filled with blackmail money from under that rock. You've been blackmailing Gene Squires."

"Why that's crazy. I did no such thing. You're way out of line. You're going to get in a lot of trouble for this."

Rivera began emptying the man's pockets and bagging each item. His right front pants pocket contained ten one-hundred-dollar bills. "I watched you take an envelope from under that rock, remove the money, and stuff it into your pocket."

"Nonsense. That's my money. It was in my pocket when I left Moab. You're making a big mistake."

"I saw what I saw."

"Well, it's your word against mine. I did no such thing."

"That crumpled envelope in your truck says differently."

"I found that lying on the road. I dislike litter, so I picked it up like any good citizen would."

Rivera extracted his cell phone and called the dispatcher. He requested she send a couple of deputies, one to pick up Broderick's vehicle and one to transport him to a jail cell. Rivera's personal pickup wasn't suitable for transporting prisoners.

"Just remember, it's your word against mine," Broderick repeated, his voice now a shout.

"You can sit while we wait."

Broderick lowered himself to the road and leaned back against his pickup.

Rivera remained standing, now reflecting on Broderick's comment. Your word against mine. He was right, of course, but the deputy knew that Squires had recorded the serial numbers of the bills. Or had he? He said he would, but he might have forgotten. Or simply decided not to cooperate. Rivera realized he should have checked with Squires this morning. But he knew he had Broderick on fraud charges as well. He fully expected to find evidence in Broderick's residence that he'd received proof of Squire's infidelity weeks ago without telling his client. There was also the matter of Derek's murder.

"We'll also be looking into the matter of fraud," said Rivera. He wanted to keep the conversation going while he waited for the deputies to arrive. Anything Broderick said might be helpful in rounding out the logic of his case.

"That's ridiculous. I haven't committed fraud. I'm a good citizen with a clean record. Where are you getting all this stuff?"

"I'm talking about withholding information from a client—Ginny Hempstead—to keep the fees coming in, information that would have been sufficient to meet her needs."

"That's your opinion. I felt we needed more info, so we'd have a rock-solid case in court. Who the hell are you to tell me how I should run my business?"

"And we'll be checking your firearms to learn whether or not you're also a murderer."

"What? Are you crazy? I've never killed anyone in my life. Are you talking about Derek?"

"You had a motive."

"God, this is a nightmare." Broderick's eyes were becoming moist with anger. "You're accusing me of all kinds of things I didn't do. You're gonna ruin my life."

"Derek was killed on Tuesday morning. Can you account for your time that day?

"Yes, dammit. I was in Cortez that morning, visiting a Ford dealership. I was thinking about buying a new truck."

"That can easily be checked. What was the salesperson's name?"

"I don't remember. She was blonde. I gave her one of my cards."

While he waited, Rivera began thinking about all the things that could go wrong with this case. What if he'd figured everything incorrectly? What if Squires hadn't recorded the serial numbers of the bills? And what if Squires denied he left the bills under the rock out of fear that Ginny Hempstead might learn he was paying someone to keep his extramarital affair secret. She would reason that if he weren't cheating, there would have been no blackmail payments. And what if Ginny had agreed that one video of Squires and his girlfriend wasn't enough to guarantee the legal outcome she wanted? Lastly, what if Rivera was wrong about Broderick having killed Derek to prevent him from revealing Broderick's fraud scheme? What if it had been someone else? Rivera fully intended to check with the dealership to see if there was any record of Broderick having been there.

During the next several hours, Broderick was booked and placed in a jail cell. As soon as the paperwork was finished, Rivera called Gene Squires on his cell phone.

The phone rang but there was no answer. Rivera's stomach muscles tightened.

After four rings, the answering machine came on. It gave the usual greeting, followed by *Please leave a message at the tone.*

"This is Deputy Rivera. Call me as soon as possible. It's important." He left his cell phone number in case Squires had misplaced his card.

Rivera hung up, feeling frustrated.

Thirty minutes later, his phone rang. "This is Gene Squires. Sorry I missed your call. I was doing some laps on the high school track. My phone was in the car."

"Did you record the serial numbers of those hundred-dollar bills like I asked you to?"

"Um, well, no I didn't. To be honest, I was afraid I'd get all mixed up in a prosecution, and my wife would learn things I didn't want her to know. You can understand that."

"No, I don't understand that at all." Rivera clicked off, kicking himself for not recording the serial numbers himself right after Squires had placed the envelope under the rock. Now it looked like the case would hinge on Rivera's word against Broderick's. Squires could deny that he'd ever paid blackmail money or had any involvement with Broderick at all. And Broderick could stick to his story that the money was in his pocket when he left Moab, and the crumpled envelope was the result of a good citizen doing his duty and keeping the backcountry clean. Then where would Rivera be? Certainly not in a strong position. At least he had his periodic status calls to the dispatcher to back up his story. And if need be, he could try to persuade Elizabeth Blackstone to testify that Squires had told her he was being blackmailed. Perhaps Ginny Hempstead would be willing to testify that she hired Broderick to spy on Squires and prove his infidelity.

Fortunately, a judge was persuaded that there was sufficient circumstantial evidence to justify expedited search warrants for Broderick's home and vehicle, as Broderick not only was seen retrieving the blackmail money by a respected deputy, but also had a motive for killing Derek Webster.

At Broderick's home, a collection of thumb drives was found next to his computer. They contained the same videos that were stored in Derek's computer. One contained the explicit evidence of Squires's infidelity that Rivera had seen in Derek's videos. Rivera now had proof of fraud and probable proof of blackmail, but no proof of murder.

There were no firearms found in his pickup. Two rifles and four handguns were found in his home and later tested. As it turned out, none was a match for the bullet which had killed Derek Webster. That came as a bit of a surprise to Rivera, as Broderick had a clear motive to eliminate Derek. Nevertheless, Rivera would continue to investigate the possibility that Broderick was the shooter.

He called the Ford dealership in Cortez and asked if there was a blonde salesperson working there. He explained that he needed to confirm something with her, without going into a long explanation. Fortunately, he received a straightforward answer. "We have two blondes working here. One's on duty now and the other is on a hike in Cedar Mesa. She and some friends are exploring Owl Canyon. She won't be back till Sunday around noon."

Rivera spoke with the blonde on duty and learned that she did not recognize Broderick's name, nor did she receive a business card from a private investigator. She said she would have Susie Reynolds, the other blonde, call Rivera when she returned. Reynolds would be unreachable by cell phone until she came out of that canyon.

30

RIVERA SAT IN Sheriff Louise Anderson's office, giving her a rundown on what had transpired in the Broderick matter. When he finished, she sat there thinking.

"So you've got him on fraud and blackmail, but what about the Derek Webster homicide? Do you think Broderick was the shooter?"

"We tested his guns. None of them was used in the shooting."

"He might have tossed a gun into the river."

"True, but he claims to have been at a Ford dealership in Cortez at the time Derek was killed. I'm trying to verify his story."

"If it wasn't Broderick, then who else had a motive?"

"That's the problem. Judging by the life Derek led, he was the kind of guy everyone liked. His one questionable activity was his drone business. Spying on people was the only part of his life where I could see him making enemies."

"Isn't it possible he had another assignment that he didn't log into his journal?"

"Maybe," said Rivera, giving the question some thought. "If you're thinking he might have been involved in some nefarious enterprise, that's possible, but it doesn't seem consistent with his character."

"Maybe there was a dark side to his life. Something you haven't uncovered yet."

"That's possible too."

"Someone had a reason to kill him. If not Broderick, then who?"

Rivera shrugged. "I don't know."

"Well, Broderick is probably our man. The facts seem to keep pointing in his direction. But we need hard proof. Keep digging and let me know what you find out."

Rivera stood up. "Any word yet from the DEA on their peyote investigation?"

Anderson smiled. "Nothing yet. You stick to the Derek Webster case, okay? Let Agent Masters and the DEA worry about the peyote business."

Rivera returned to his office and closed the door. Just hearing the name Masters rankled him. Now he wanted more than ever to break Masters's case for him and maybe deflate his ego a notch or two. He stewed in those thoughts for a while, then forced his thinking back to the Derek Webster matter. The 'Broderick did it' theory was the only sensible possibility that presented itself, but there was something fundamental about the theory that had been bothering him all along. The amount of money involved in the fraud and blackmail schemes didn't seem to be sufficient to warrant murder. It wasn't even enough for Broderick to buy a new Ford truck. Maybe there was another angle that Rivera was missing.

His stomach growled, reminding him it was time for dinner. He decided to call it a day and head home. Maybe some food and a good night's sleep would clear his head and help him come up with some fresh insights on the case.

31

RIVERA AWOKE EARLY, showered, dressed, and headed for the Rim Rock Diner for his usual breakfast. He didn't have the pleasure of Betty's company as she only worked on weekdays. His waitress today was Henrietta, a middle-aged woman who was polite and efficient, but not nearly as entertaining as Betty.

When he arrived at the office, no new information was available from Phil Broderick as he had lawyered up and become silent. There was nothing more Rivera could do on the fraud and blackmail charges, and the question of murder could not be advanced until Susie Reynolds from the Ford dealership returned his call. He decided to switch gears while he waited and drive out to Cisco to question Jimmy Ventner, the peyote source Bill Toliver had identified.

Rivera was concerned he was on the verge of getting himself in trouble. To cover himself, if only slightly, he called Emmett Mitchell with the intention of proposing that their peyote collaboration be extended.

"Manny, what are you doing working? It's Sunday morning, and we're getting ready for church."

"I've learned the identity of the man who was the source of the peyote that made Abigail Nolan sick. His name is Jimmy Ventner."

"Which means you talked to that other kid, what was his name?"

"Bill Toliver. I didn't talk to him directly. I used a reliable intermediary."

"Oh, Manny. You're going to get yourself in big trouble."

"If I'm questioned, all I need to say is that you asked me to interview Ventner as a follow up to the peyote case in your county."

"But I haven't asked you to do that."

"Not yet, you haven't."

"I understand what you're asking me to do—be a party to deceiving the DEA. And if I accede to your wishes, maybe we could share a jail cell."

"I think it's a legitimate action. You're interested in Abigail Nolan's peyote use, the Abigail Nolan from your own San Juan County, and you request that I interview one Jimmy Ventner of Grand County who supplied said peyote. Meanwhile, per instructions from the DEA, I'll be avoiding the Lucia Navarro case altogether."

"The DEA won't see it that way."

"I know."

There was a long pause, during which Rivera heard the voices of kids in the background. "Okay, consider it done. I'm asking you to interview the Ventner kid. Now, I've got to get going or we'll be late for church."

"Thanks, Emmett. One more thing. Did Sheriff Zilic report Abigail Nolan's peyote sickness to the DEA?"

"No. It wasn't a big enough deal. And besides, you know how he feels about the feds."

"Great. Thanks."

That bit of information was a relief to Rivera. If a second peyote incident in southeast Utah came to the attention of the DEA, it was likely to bring Agent Masters to town, a distraction he didn't need right now.

Rivera left the office and drove out of Moab, headed for Cisco. He turned onto Hwy 128 and headed upriver. After crossing the Dewey Bridge, the sight of the Webster Nursery reminded him of the look on Hal Webster's face when Rivera told him his son was dead.

The drive to Cisco gave Rivera time to think. His objective was to find an answer to Lucia's father's question about the source of the peyote and do so without getting crossways with the DEA or Sheriff Anderson. Rivera knew that it wasn't really important that Mr. Navarro learn the source of the peyote. It wouldn't bring his daughter back. But at least it would tell him that the authorities had considered the matter important enough to investigate.

The next logical step in that pursuit was to interview Jimmy Ventner and find out where *he* got the peyote.

Despite what Jimmy revealed, Rivera couldn't arrest him since that would make it obvious he had violated the DEA's orders. So his conversation with Jimmy would be just that—a conversation. Private and unofficial. Hopefully *very* private. He knew he was on thin ice, but he felt driven to get an answer for Mr. Navarro.

Soon Rivera could see Cisco in the distance. He knew it well, having visited many times on law enforcement matters and as an interested civilian driven by curiosity. In its heyday, Cisco was a place along the old Denver and Rio Grande Western Railroad where steam locomotives stopped to replenish their water supply. A small town grew up alongside the railroad with a hotel, a saloon, a general store, and a few individual residences. In the 1960s, when steam locomotives were phased out in favor of diesels, Cisco was all but abandoned and became one of Utah's many ghost towns. It began a resurrection when people, starting with hippies from the 1960s and 1970s, began inhabiting the old, abandoned buildings, rebuilding and painting them and planting gardens. It evolved into an interesting little community which had a striking view of the LaSal Mountains and was populated with free thinking, independent people.

Rivera turned right on the gravel road which led into the community and stopped. He pulled from his shirt pocket the map that Chris Carey had drawn for him and studied it. He followed its directions, driving three blocks straight ahead, turning left, then one block and a right turn onto a dead-end dirt road. The only house in view was located at the far end of the road. It was a one-story white clapboard affair with an old maroon pickup parked in front. Rivera pulled up behind the pickup and stopped.

Next to the house was a corrugated metal shed filled with tools and an old pickup resting on cinderblocks. The yard had been left natural and was filled with snakeweed now blooming with tiny yellow flowers. About forty yards behind the house was a brush arbor, a small structure with open sides that was topped off with brush to provide a shady place to sit. Two canvas chairs sat in the arbor. Farther back was what appeared to be a small Navajo hogan under construction. It was an octagonal structure made of repurposed wood planks and had been completed only to a height of four feet, obviously a work in progress. When completed, it would serve as someone's home. Its door was correctly facing eastward, consistent with the Navajo belief that, upon awakening in the morning, the first thing one should see is the rising sun. A greeting-the-day ritual would follow. To the right of the hogan was a small half dome structure made from mud reinforced with straw and tree branches. Rivera recognized it as a sweat lodge, a sight one occasionally saw on the reservation.

The deputy assumed all this was the work of Jimmy Ventner, the young man Toliver described as an Indian wannabe. Rivera got out of his vehicle and approached the front door of the house. Halfway there, the door flew open, and a young boy came bounding out. He appeared to be five or six years old and was headed Rivera's way. The deputy stopped.

"Hi, Mister. My name's Rodney." He had blond hair with a pronounced cowlick and was wearing shorts and a T-shirt. He was carrying a stuffed giraffe, so worn that the stuffing was visible through openings worn through the outer skin.

"Well, hi there, Rodney. How are you today?"

"Fine. My daddy's taking a shower. He'll be out soon." The boy held the giraffe up for Rivera to see.

"Does your giraffe have a name?"

"Jerry."

Rivera smiled. "Hello, Jerry the Giraffe."

The boy grinned broadly. "My Uncle Jimmy gave him to me. I've had him for a long time."

"Is your uncle Jimmy Ventner?"

The boy nodded, looking up at Rivera with pride.

"Is he at home? I'd like to talk with him."

"No. Uncle Jimmy went to pick up some wood."

Just then, the front door opened and a man wearing jeans and a T-shirt came outside. He was drying his hair with a towel. He had a concerned look on his face. "Is everything okay, Deputy?"

"Everything is fine. I was looking for Jimmy Ventner. I'd like to talk with him."

"He's not here right now. He went to Moab where an old house is being torn down to see if he could pick up some scrap lumber for a hogan he's building out back. I'm Charles, his older brother. Is there a problem?"

"I'd just like to ask him a few questions. What time do you expect him back?"

"He left about three hours ago, so I expect him back pretty soon."

"I'll wait, then."

Moments later, an old gray pickup truck turned onto the road leading to the house. It stopped fifty yards away and remained stationary for a long moment. Rivera figured the driver was Jimmy Ventner, and he was sizing up the situation, deciding whether to continue or run. The pickup then resumed its forward motion and drove up to the house. The bed of the truck was filled with used planks, plywood, and two-by-fours.

"There's my Uncle Jimmy," said Rodney, jumping up and down and pointing.

Ventner got out of his vehicle, and the boy ran to him and hugged his leg. Ventner hugged him back. "I got us a good load of lumber, Rodney. We can build the hogan a little bit higher today."

He was a thin man with a friendly face who looked to be in his mid-twenties. He too was wearing jeans and a T-shirt, but he had the added accoutrement of a red headband. A faded pair of red and black stripes were barely visible on each cheek. Rivera imagined that he applied fresh paint only when consuming peyote with his friends during which time he referred to himself as the Peyote Chief.

"Yá' át' ééh, Deputy. What's up?"

"I'd like to ask you a few questions." Rivera turned to Charles. "Charles, would you and Rodney excuse us? This needs to be a private conversation."

"Sure," said Charles. "Let's go inside, Rodney." They turned and left, the boy holding his father's hand and looking back at Rivera with a confused expression.

"What's this about?" asked Jimmy.

Rivera waited until the others were inside. He saw no point in beating around the bush. "This is about the peyote you've been providing to your friends from school. I'm not here to arrest you. In fact, I'd like to keep our conversation just between the two of us. I'm simply looking for some information about your source."

Ventner smiled and seemed almost unconcerned. "Let's go sit under the brush arbor and get out of the sun."

"Good idea."

As they walked toward the brush arbor, Jimmy explained to Rivera why he was building a hogan. "I have a great deal of respect for the Navajo culture. I want to live my life the way they do. So when the hogan is finished, it will be my home. Charles doesn't mind my being here. In fact, he welcomes it. There aren't many young kids living in Cisco, so I serve as a kind of playmate for Rodney. When Carol died—she was Charles's wife—he asked me to move in so we could share babysitting duties for Rodney. It's worked out great, but I'd like a place of my own."

"Have you always had an interest in the Navajo culture?"

"Yes, ever since I can remember. Father took Charles, my sister Sarah, and I to the rez many times when we were kids. He sold school supplies to the Navajos. I admired the people, their value system, and their philosophy of life. I guess I wanted to be just like them. I didn't do well in school. The teachers said I was different and had attention deficit disorder. Maybe I did. I'm not sure. But I know my interests were way different from regular kids. I don't have much and I've never wanted much. I'm happy and I don't care about getting rich. I just want to enjoy life while I'm on this earth, however short a time that might be."

They reached the brush arbor and sat down in chairs facing the mountains. Rivera relaxed, enjoying the shade and the view. Jimmy started talking before Rivera could ask a question. He explained that peyote was used in religious ceremonies of the Native American Church, that its use was considered a sacrament, and that it produced a state of mind that enabled members of the congregation to better bond with one another.

As Rivera listened, he sized up Jimmy as a likeable person but one who marched to the beat of a different drummer as compared to others his age. The deputy found himself becoming intrigued with the young man.

"Many Navajos belong to the Native American Church," said Jimmy, "so I became interested in it. I applied for membership about a year ago. Unfortunately, I haven't been accepted yet. I keep hoping I'll hear something soon as I desperately want to go on a vision quest. To experience just one vision is my main goal in life. I knew that being under the influence of peyote would greatly increase my chances of having a vision, but I didn't know how or where to get it."

Rivera had heard a little about visions among Native American peoples and was vaguely familiar with the concept. As he recalled, a vision was some kind of important revelation granted to only a few lucky souls. It usually involved fasting and remaining alone for days at some sacred site selected by the elders in the hopes that one's purpose in life would be revealed to them. Peyote was said to enhance the chances of success.

"Then I learned recently from a friend that I could get peyote locally. So I jumped at the chance."

Rivera sat up straight. "Where can you get it locally?"

"First let me say that I never sold the stuff. I only used it myself and shared it with a few friends. I wanted to see if we would better relate to one another, like the members of the Native American Church."

"So where did you get the peyote?"

"At the Webster Nursery. They grow it in the greenhouses."

Rivera left Jimmy at the brush arbor and headed back to his vehicle. Jimmy's brother Charles was waiting for him there.

"Is Jimmy in any kind of trouble?"

"We'll see."

"Is this visit about his using peyote?"

Rivera looked at him. "What do you know about that?"

"My brother has late-stage glioblastoma. He says his peyote use is ceremonial and he hopes it will help him achieve a vision, but privately he tells me it also helps with the pain."

"Glio...I'm not familiar with that term."

"Glioblastoma. It's a type of brain cancer. Usually terminal."

"I'm sorry to hear that."

"When his final day comes, little Rodney will be devastated. So will I."

32

RIVERA LEFT THE Ventner compound in a hurry and headed back on Hwy 128 toward the Webster Nursery. His mind was buzzing with questions as he tried to wrap his brain around what he had just learned. Was there a linkage between Derek Webster's death and peyote cultivation at the Webster Nursery? Had Derek been killed because of some drug related matter? Had Rivera totally misjudged him and been on the wrong track all along? The sound of his tires rumbling on the shoulder of the road and the pinging of gravel against his vehicle's undercarriage forced him to slow down and concentrate on keeping his pickup on the pavement.

Rivera's cell phone buzzed. He jerked it from his shirt pocket, irritated by the interruption of his thoughts.

"Hello?"

"Hello. Is this Deputy Rivera?"

"Yes, it is."

"This is Susie Reynolds with the Ford dealership in Cortez. I understand you wanted to talk to me."

"Yes, thanks for the call. I'm interested in a visit you might have had from Phil Broderick last Tuesday. Can you confirm that he was there?"

"Oh, yes. He was definitely here. He's interested in buying a new pickup truck. Hold on and let me make sure that was Tuesday."

Rivera heard the turning of pages. "Yes, it was Tuesday."

"Do you remember what time of day he was there?"

"It was in the morning. I get here at nine o'clock. He came about thirty minutes later."

"Okay, thank you very much."

"While I have you on the phone, would you have any interest in buying a new Ford?"

"No, not today, thanks. Appreciate the help."

Another new piece of information, thought Rivera. Broderick could not have been Derek Webster's killer. He was over a hundred miles away when the fatal shot was fired. He was a fraudster and a blackmailer, but not a killer. As Rivera drove, he realized he had been dealing with two separate cases all along. One was Broderick's financial shenanigans with Ginny Hempstead and Gene Squires, and the other was the murder of Derek Webster, possibly related to the drug operation at the Webster Nursery.

He turned into the nursery and parked in front of Hal Webster's house. He exited his vehicle just as Webster opened the door and stepped onto the porch. His eyes were bloodshot, and his face seemed to sag. He nodded to Rivera without smiling.

"I heard you drive up. Any news on who shot my son?"

"No. I'm afraid not. We're still working on it."

"Do we know if it was an accident? I'd hate to think my son had any enemies."

"No, it's still under investigation."

Webster nodded his understanding. "How can I help you today, Deputy?"

Rivera no longer felt constrained in asking questions about peyote, despite the mandate of the DEA. Now he had a legitimate interest in openly pursuing the peyote angle, since it appeared to be related to a murder he was investigating. "I'm here to talk about peyote. I understand you've been growing it in your greenhouses."

Webster looked confused. "Say what?"

"Peyote."

"Deputy, I don't know what you're talking about. We don't grow peyote here. You're welcome to take a look, but that's the craziest thing I've ever heard."

"Mind coming with me?"

"Let's go." Webster walked with a purposeful stride toward the greenhouses. "Why the hell would I be growing peyote?" he said, almost to himself.

They entered the first greenhouse and Rivera began a search of the plants growing there. The interior was humid and had the pleasant fragrance of fresh soil and peat. Webster led Rivera up and down each aisle, pointing to plants and naming them as they walked. There were bougainvilleas, poinsettias, amaryllises, mistletoe, small holly berry plants, orchids, and many others. There were also boxes of Christmas cactus, aloe vera plants, and tiny prickly pear cactus, but no peyote.

They repeated the process in the second greenhouse. It contained mostly leafy plants. There were philodendrons, rubber plants, fiddle leaf figs, scheffleras, jade plants, bromeliads, and many others, but no peyote.

The third greenhouse looked less organized than the first two. It was cluttered with piles of mulch, tools, long tables with assorted plants and flowers, boxes of seedlings, a few small trees, stacks of plastic pots, and bags of peat moss and fertilizer. Toward the rear was a collection of a hundred or so individual cactuses, one or a few of each type. Some were small like barrel cactus and Madagascar palm, others were tall, like ocotillo and cholla. Webster gestured toward them. "This is Guy Richardson's personal cactus collection. He's a member of the Moab Succulent Club, and they all enjoy growing cactuses that don't normally survive in Utah. Of course, they do fine in a greenhouse environment where the temperature is controlled."

Rivera stopped and carefully inspected the collection, one cactus at a time. No peyote.

Against the back wall was a set of metal shelves that went from the floor almost to the ceiling. They contained supplies such as gloves, peat cups, sacks of grass seed, planters, and bags of tulip bulbs. High on the top shelf were two flat wooden boxes.

Rivera pointed. "What's in those wooden boxes on top?"

"I have no idea. Could be anything. We've been accumulating stuff in here for over thirty years. I'm in no shape to climb up there and look. You'll have to do that yourself."

Rivera laid his hat on a bench and began climbing, using the shelves as steps. When he was high enough, he peered into the boxes. Each contained a bed of soil and a half-dozen peyote cactuses. He held on to the shelving with one hand and used the other to grab a box and pass it down to Webster.

Webster placed it on a table, inspected the contents, and shook his head. "What the hell?"

Rivera passed the other box down and lowered himself to the floor. The two men stared at the plants, then each other.

"Damn," said Webster, his shoulders slumping. "They look like peyote cactuses."

"That's what they are. Can you explain why they're in your greenhouse?"

"No, I can't. I have no idea why they're here. I'll have to ask Guy about it when he gets back. He left several hours ago to make some deliveries in Grand Junction."

"Is he your only employee?"

"Right now, yes. We hire transient labor during the planting and growing season, but this time of year it's just me and Guy." Webster appeared to be getting mad as he digested the situation.

"And you've never seen this before?"

"I already told you I haven't."

"Maybe Guy put them up there." Rivera presented the idea as a question.

"He damn well better not have."

They left the boxes of peyote in the greenhouse and walked outside, just as a Webster Nursery truck pulled into the yard and stopped. Guy Richardson shut off the engine, stepped out of the truck, and waved at the two men.

33

HAL WEBSTER WALKED over to Guy Richardson and faced him squarely. "Tell me about that peyote you've been growing in greenhouse number three."

Richardson's smile faded and he was silent for a long moment. He meekly shrugged. "I'm sorry, Hal. I didn't mean to cause you any trouble. I should have told you about it long ago. You know how interested I am in different cactus types and how they grow and bloom and reproduce. It's been a hobby of mine for a long time. Well, years ago I read an article about peyote and got curious about it. I just wanted to see if I could grow it. I thought about planting them in the woods on the other side of the river, but there's no way they could survive the Utah winters. So I grew them in the greenhouse and kept them out of sight. I didn't see the harm in it. I'm really sorry, Hal."

"Didn't see the harm in it? You may have destroyed my business. I can't believe you would do something like that, Guy. After all these years of working together, I feel betrayed. This is totally unacceptable."

"Hal, are you saying you're firing me?"

Webster's face softened and his gaze fell to the ground. He shook his head. "Uh, well, I guess not, Guy. I'd be lost out here without you."

Rivera decided it was time to step in. "Where did you get the peyote to begin with?"

"I bought them seven or eight years ago from a guy who lives in Montezuma Creek. He's a Navajo whose uncle lives on the rez. The uncle is a member of the Native American Church so it's legal for him to acquire and use peyote. He's responsible for the acquisition and storage of peyote for his church community, so he has no trouble getting the stuff. I bought a dozen peyote cactuses and planted them in those wooden boxes. I knew I wasn't supposed to have them, but I couldn't resist the chance to add them to my collection."

"What's the name of the guy in Montezuma Creek who sold you the peyote?"

"Tommy Redhorse. I haven't seen him since I made the original purchase, but I get a call from him about once a year offering to sell me more peyote. I never bought any more from him because the originals are doing just fine."

Rivera jotted the name into his notepad. "Have you tried it yourself?"

"No. I don't do drugs. Never have."

"I noticed some of the buttons have been sliced off. Since you haven't used any yourself, does that mean you've been selling it?"

"I've never sold any. I've given some away."

"To whom?"

"We have a Succulent Club in Moab. It's for people interested in growing succulents and especially cactuses. It's a small club, only about a dozen members. We try to grow plants not indigenous to the Moab area—things like ocotillo, lechuguilla, candelilla, and so forth. It's always a thrill whenever one of them blooms. Especially the ocotillo. Anyway, there's a guy in the club who kept asking me if I knew where he could get some peyote. I made the mistake of hinting I knew a source. He kept bugging me, so finally I gave in and told him I had some. He got all excited and asked for a few of them. I told him no, that I didn't want to part with any of them. He asked me if it was possible to grow them from cuttings. I said yes, I believe so. He said he wanted to try to grow some from cuttings. After much pestering, I caved in and cut off some buttons for him. I made him promise to keep it all private. But I suspect he used the buttons to get high instead of planting them."

"What's his name?"

"Jimmy Ventner."

Hal Webster looked at Rivera. His eyes were watery. "Are you through with me?"

"Yes, for now," said Rivera.

Webster started walking back to his house without saying another word.

Richardson walked after him. "Hal, I'm not a dealer. Honest. I didn't do anything wrong."

"This nursery has a good reputation. You helped build that reputation. Now you've torn it down." Webster continued walking to his house, leaving Richardson standing there with a sad expression.

Rivera had a decision to make. Should he arrest Guy Richardson? What kind of case did he have? A man who loves plants acquires some peyote, plants it, watches it grow, and receives some enjoyment in the process. Then he gives some cuttings away to a fellow member of the Moab Succulents Club, believing he too had a botanical interest. So where's the crime? Simply in having peyote in one's possession in the first place? Rivera wasn't sure how he felt about all that, but there was one thing he was sure of. He still had no sensible idea about who had a motive to kill Derek, and whether that tied in with the peyote business. And if it did, how did that work? What was the connection?

"Did Derek know about the peyote you were growing here?"

"No. I'm sure he didn't. If he knew, he'd have made me get rid of it."

"Was he aware of your connection with a source of peyote?"

"Not to my knowledge."

Rivera considered the possibility that Derek could have accidentally discovered them in the greenhouse when he lived at the nursery but rejected that idea because of the difficulty he would have had in climbing to the top of the shelves.

"Let's keep our conversation private for now. Discuss it with no one." Rivera didn't want the DEA to learn of the peyote growing at the nursery until after he solved the Derek Webster murder case. If they knew about it now, they would only get in the way.

Richardson looked relieved. "Okay. So I'm not under arrest?"

"For the time being, no."

"Thank God."

"But you've got some mending to do with Hal."

"I know."

Rivera confiscated the boxes of peyote, loaded them into his vehicle, and drove out of the nursery. He reflected on what he had just done. Or didn't do. He neither arrested Guy Richardson nor Jimmy Ventner, despite both admitting to having been in possession of peyote. And the reason he didn't was because he still couldn't see the tie-in with Derek's murder and didn't want to muddy the water by getting the DEA involved. Another peyote incident in Moab would certainly bring them to his doorstep.

Rivera headed back into town, wondering if the information he'd uncovered about Tommy Redhorse and his uncle selling peyote from the Navajo Reservation would be of interest to the DEA. Perhaps the uncle was a key to solving the DEA's investigation. Rivera would sure enjoy breaking Agent Masters's case for him.

34

RIVERA RETURNED TO his office, noting that Sheriff Anderson was in her office, working on a Sunday. He went down the hallway and knocked on her door.

"Working on Sunday, Sheriff?"

"Just catching up on some paperwork."

"I'm glad you're here. I need to get you caught up on some important matters."

She set aside the file she was reading and removed her glasses. Rivera knew he was on thin ice. She'd told him to stay away from the peyote business, yet his briefing was going to be full of peyote references.

He sat down.

"Something new on the Derek Webster case?" she asked.

"There's been an interesting wrinkle. You told me to avoid the Lucia Navarro peyote matter, but it turns out there might be a connection between peyote and Derek's murder."

Her eyes narrowed. "Oh, really? What's the connection?"

"Guy Richardson, the foreman at the Webster Nursery has been growing peyote cactus in one of the greenhouses for years. I confiscated it and stored it in the evidence locker. The guy's not a user. He has a strong interest in cactus, how they grow, how they bloom, how they reproduce, and so forth, but he did cut off some buds for an acquaintance."

"Now wait a damn minute. How did you get involved in this after I gave you explicit instructions to stay away from the peyote business? I don't need the DEA hassling us."

"It's kind of complicated."

She shook her head. "I'll bet. Explain. And this better be good."

"There was a second case of peyote use I learned about a couple of days ago. A teenage girl who lives in San Juan County tried it and got sick. She ended up in the hospital. Emmett Mitchell called me and told me about it. He asked her where she'd gotten the stuff and she said from a boy in Moab named Bill Toliver. In order to comply with the instructions we received from the DEA, I didn't interview Toliver."

"Yes, go ahead. I have a feeling I'm not going to like what's coming next."

Rivera cleared his throat. "I asked Chris Carey to talk to him for me."

She straightened up and raised her voice. "You did what?"

"Chris is a good friend of the Toliver family. He's known the Toliver boy since the day he was born."

"We're going to have some explaining to do to Masters and the DEA." There was a long pause as if she was picturing how that conversation might go. "So what did Carey learn?"

"He learned that a group of U.S.U. students got together in the mountains one evening and tried peyote. The guy who brought the peyote was named Jimmy Ventner. He lives in Cisco at his brother's place."

"Have you talked with Ventner?"

"Yes, in Cisco. He's an interesting character. An Indian wannabe. Long straight hair, a red bandana, and stripes painted on his face. Behind his brother's house, he's built a brush arbor and a sweat lodge, and a small hogan is under construction. He was open about where he got the peyote. He said it came from the Webster Nursery. So that's the connection between Derek Webster's murder and the peyote business. Ventner also said he was the provider of peyote for the party that led to Lucia Navarro's accident. He felt real bad about that but said it wasn't his fault—she was there under her own volition."

"My word. I assume you paid a visit to the nursery."

"Right. Turns out Mr. Webster knew nothing about it. His foreman was growing peyote cactuses in the back of one of the greenhouses, up high on a shelf where Mr. Webster couldn't see them. The foreman's name is Guy Richardson. He's been growing peyote there for years. He's not a user. His interest is strictly botanical. He's a member of the Moab Succulents Club along with Ventner. Somehow Ventner learned about the peyote and persisted in asking Richardson for some. Richardson finally gave in."

"Anything else?"

"Richardson said he's had the peyote cactuses for seven or eight years. He told me his source for the peyote was a Navajo named Tommy Redhorse who lives in Montezuma Creek. His uncle handles peyote purchases for the Native American Church on his part of the reservation."

She smiled. "That's interesting."

"I thought so. What's even more interesting is that Tommy calls Richardson about once a year to see if he wants to buy more. So he's still in business."

"I need to call Agent Masters right away to see if he's privy to that information."

Rivera grinned. "I think we should wait. I wouldn't want the DEA to do anything that would interfere with my investigation."

She chuckled. "Very funny. But we have to tell them."

"I know."

She picked up her phone. "I have Agent Masters's cell phone number on speed dial. I'll put this call on the speakerphone so you can hear his reaction. She called Masters and waited.

"Masters here."

"This is Sheriff Louise Anderson of Grand County, Utah."

"Well, hello Sheriff. How can I help you today?"

"I have Deputy Sheriff Manny Rivera with me in the office. We're on my speakerphone. He has some information you might be interested in."

"Hello, Deputy."

Rivera detected a change in Masters's tone, as though speaking with the deputy was going to be a most distasteful experience. He made no effort to hide his disdain for Rivera. "Hello, Agent Masters. I ran across some information that might relate to your investigation of illegal peyote sales."

"I thought I told you people to stay away from anything related to peyote," he said in a loud voice. "I don't want you screwing up my investigation." Now he was almost yelling. "What part of *stay away* don't you understand?"

Rivera noticed Anderson was smiling. "Are you saying you don't want the information?" asked Rivera in the most innocent sounding voice he could muster.

"Well, no, I'm not saying that. I'm just saying...Oh, never mind. What have you got?"

"I'm investigating a murder which took place in the LaSal Mountains five days ago. The father of the victim owns a nursery. One of the workers at the nursery was growing some peyote cactuses in one of the greenhouses. His interest is botanical only. He's neither a user nor a seller. He said he bought the cactus seven or eight years ago from a Navajo named Tommy Redhorse." Rivera recited the rest of the information he had about the annual sales calls and the uncle who was a peyote buyer for the Native American Church.

There was a long pause on the line. "That's very interesting, but how did you get on the peyote trail to begin with?"

"Just stumbled across it while investigating the murder case."

"Yeah, sure, Rivera. You just stumbled across it. You're not very good at following orders, are you?"

Despite his efforts to control himself, Rivera could feel anger rising within him. Masters always had that effect on him.

Sheriff Anderson responded before Rivera could. "Now wait just a damn minute, Masters. Deputy Rivera may have just handed you your case on a silver platter. Maybe you should be showing a little gratitude."

There was a long pause. "Is Redhorse one word or two?"

35

IT WAS LATE Sunday night and Rivera spent the next hour in his office updating his report with the new discoveries of the day. He'd unveiled a tenuous link between peyote and Derek's death, but not a cause and effect. He would have to dig some more and explore that connection further.

There was one good outcome from today's efforts. He now had an answer to Emiliano Navarro's question about where Lucia had gotten the peyote. He looked at his watch. It was still early enough to pay him a visit and let him know that the law enforcement community was actively pursuing Lucia's case and had always been doing so. Maybe he could accomplish one good deed before calling it a day.

He drove to the address he had for Mr. Navarro. It was a modest home on the west side of Moab with a yard that hadn't received much love. He parked, noting the lights in the house were on. He knocked on the door.

Mr. Navarro opened the door and squinted at Rivera.

Rich Curtin

"Hello, Deputy." There was a smell of liquor on his breath, and he looked like he hadn't showered in days. The man's pain was palpable, and Rivera felt a deep sense of sorrow.

"May I come in? I have some information for you."

"Navarro stepped back and gestured for Rivera to enter."

The deputy sat in an upholstered chair and Navarro sat on the couch. On the coffee table between them was a framed photograph of Lucia, an open photo album, an assortment of loose individual photos, a bottle of Jack Daniels, and a glass partially filled with an amber liquid. Rivera glanced around the room at the sparse furnishings: a television, an ottoman pushed against the wall, a coat rack by the door with work clothing hanging on it, and a set of shelves containing paperback novels and several porcelain statues. A crucifix and two framed pictures of cities in Old Mexico hung on the walls.

Rivera was uncomfortable being in the home of a man who had just lost his child. Navarro's sadness was palpable. Lucia used to live here with him—now she was gone forever. Rivera's goal was to satisfy the man's need for information about the circumstances surrounding his daughter's death and hopefully erase any bad impressions the father had about local law enforcement.

Navarro picked up the framed photograph of Lucia and held it out so Rivera could see it. She had long dark hair and was wearing a fancy gown.

"This photo was taken the night she went to her high school prom."

Rivera studied the photo. "She was a beautiful young lady."

"Yes, she was." Navarro looked at his daughter for a long moment, then held the photo to his heart. He placed it on the table and sat there, staring at Rivera as if waiting for him to say something.

Rivera composed his thoughts and began. "I'm sorry to intrude on you at a time like this, but I wanted to give you some straight answers. During your visits to the sheriff's office after Lucia died, we were unable to answer your questions about where she had gotten the peyote. That's because the federal government was conducting a larger investigation into the illegal use of peyote. They instructed our office to keep out of it for fear we might do something that would hinder their investigation. They also instructed us not to mention that they were investigating the matter. So all those times you visited the sheriff's office, I was unable to satisfy you, to give you a complete answer, to assure you that an investigation was underway." Rivera stopped and waited.

Navarro took a sip of bourbon and said nothing. He just stared at Rivera and slowly nodded. His eyes seemed glazed over, and Rivera wondered if he was paying attention.

"Do you understand that?" asked Rivera.

"Yes."

Rich Curtin

"Well, now I can answer the question you asked during all those visits. The peyote Lucia took was from the Webster Nursery. They were growing it because of a general interest in cactuses. Someone took some of it to a party Lucia was attending." Rivera waited, but Navarro said nothing as if he were numb. There seemed to be little if any reaction to what the deputy had told him.

Rivera stood up. He was brokenhearted for the man and wanted to leave as soon as he could. "I just wanted you to know that. I have to go now." He knew there was no way he could soothe the man's pain. He was once again reminded of the risk of having kids.

"Thank you for coming," managed Navarro, remaining seated.

Rivera went to the door to let himself out. As he pulled it open, the coat and hat hanging on the coat rack caught his eye. The hat had a wide, flat brim. Next to the coat rack was a twisted hickory walking stick leaning against the wall. As he stepped outside and was closing the door, he glanced back at the rack. Now he could see a long feather protruding from the hatband. The hat and walking stick reminded him of the man with the rifle walking in the canyon who had appeared in Derek's video from the day of the shooting. His mind raced to process this new information.

Could Emiliano Navarro have been the shooter? Rivera's initial impulse was to brush that thought aside, as it made no sense. Even if Navarro was capable of

244

murder—which Rivera had no reason to believe—Derek Webster wasn't involved in the peyote trade, at least as far as the deputy knew. Since he had nothing to do with Lucia's death, Navarro had no reason to kill him. But Rivera's investigative instincts pushed him in a different direction. His training and experience had taught him to leave no possible motive unexamined in conducting an investigation. The more possibilities one can logically eliminate, the closer one gets to targeting the real motive for the murder.

By the time he reached his vehicle, he had replayed that portion of the video in his mind a half-dozen times. Lots of people have walking sticks and wide brim hats for hiking. The hat for protection from the rays of the sun, more intense at the higher altitudes, and the walking stick to aid in one's balance on a rough trail. He thought about the walking stick. Most hikers would use a hiking pole—a walking stick was less common. And the long feather in the hatband was quite unusual. Yet, Derek had nothing to do with the peyote Lucia had used. Or did he? Rivera could make no sense of what he had learned.

He yawned. He was tired and needed a good night's sleep. He would consider all that some more in the morning when his mind was fresh.

36

THE MORNING SUN SLANTED through Rivera's bedroom window and woke him from a fitful sleep. He looked at the alarm clock. It was past eight o'clock and he'd overslept after tossing and turning until well past 2:00 a.m. The good night's rest he'd hoped for hadn't materialized. The thought of Emiliano Navarro killing Derek Webster had kept him awake most of the night as his mind searched for a possible motive. He considered every angle he could imagine but found none that made any sense. If the clothing on the coat rack was the same as that shown in the video, perhaps it belonged to a friend of Navarro's who had a motive. Or maybe the whole business was just a coincidence. There had to be more than one feathered hat in the hiking world.

He showered, shaved, and dressed, still evaluating the possibilities. Maybe Rivera was wrong about Derek Webster. Maybe instead of being a solid citizen who worked hard at overcoming his handicap, he was somehow involved with Guy Richardson in growing and distributing peyote. But that idea went against Rivera's assessment of Derek's character. It also made no sense in terms of the tiny quantity of peyote that Richardson was growing in the greenhouse. Was more being grown elsewhere?

In order to save time, he ate a bowl of raisin bran at home instead of going to the Rim Rock Diner for breakfast. By the time he got to work, Rivera had decided on a way to narrow down the field of possibilities. If Emiliano Navarro was the shooter and felt safe in not disposing of the clothing he was wearing during the crime, perhaps he still had the rifle he'd used that day. A search warrant would answer that question.

He went directly to Sheriff Anderson's office and explained the situation to her, noting that his request was based on a hunch and not hard evidence. He was not surprised at her pushback.

She stared at him. "So you want to search the home of a man whose daughter died in an automobile accident while under the effects of peyote, simply because you saw a familiar-looking hat and walking stick in his house. Is that what you're saying?"

"Yes. Well, the clothing on the coat rack is a match for the clothing in the video."

"But there's no hard evidence of a connection between the guy in Derek's video and the killing."

"He was in the area when it happened."

"He wasn't the only one in the area. There were other hunters there and also those archaeology people. And who knows who else. There may have been others that were not in the field of view of the drone's camera."

"How many hikers, or hunters for that matter, do you know that hike the backcountry with a tall feather stuck in their hat?"

"None I know of. But there are bound to be some. So is it your theory that Navarro killed Derek Webster for being part of the peyote trade? Is there any evidence Derek was dealing? For that matter, is there even any evidence of a peyote trade at all?"

"The DEA seems to think there is." Rivera felt like he was grasping at straws.

"Manny, I'm just not sure a judge would grant you a search warrant on the basis of such flimsy evidence."

"We could try. If the ballistics test is negative, it will save me a lot of chasing around."

"If he even owns a rifle."

"Right."

"From what I've learned about Mr. Navarro, he sounds like a good citizen."

"He might be. Probably is. But if I can eliminate him as a possibility, it will improve my chances of finding the real shooter. I won't be wasting my time pursuing him as a suspect if he's an innocent man." And maybe I'll get a good night's sleep, he thought to himself.

"Well, I guess there's no harm in trying. Write it up and let's see if it flies."

Rivera filled out the Search Warrant Affidavit form and hand carried it to the courthouse. He presented it to one of the magistrate clerks and learned that the judge wouldn't be back in his office for a couple of hours. He explained the need for the warrant and then returned to his office to sit and wait, suffering through each passing minute. Patience was not one of his virtues.

Thirty minutes later, his telephone rang. He snatched it out of its cradle, hoping it was word from the judge. Instead, the caller was Ginny Hempstead.

"Deputy Rivera, I just learned that Phil Broderick is in jail and that you're the one who put him there."

"That's correct."

"Can you tell me why? I'm concerned about the work he was doing for me."

Rivera hesitated, wondering how much he could legally tell her. After a brief mental tussle, he decided she had a right to know. Besides, arrest information was available to the public.

"He was arrested on fraud and blackmail charges."

"Really? I guess I misjudged him. I thought he was an upstanding individual. Can you give me any details?"

"As a matter of fact, both charges are related to the investigation he was conducting for you."

The pitch of her voice rose an octave. "What on earth do you mean?"

"He had incontrovertible proof of your husband's infidelity weeks ago. I've seen the video myself. He didn't inform you so he could continue receiving your weekly payments."

"My word! I had no idea. What about the blackmail?"

"Broderick was also blackmailing Gene Squires to remain silent about what he knew. So he was collecting money from both ends."

"So the proof I was looking for currently exists?"

"Yes. We can't release it just yet, but we will as soon as we can."

"Thank you. I appreciate that. I don't want to view the video, but are you sure it's incontrovertible evidence?"

"Oh yes, I'm sure."

After the phone call, Rivera finished typing his report. Now he sat there wondering what his next step would be if the judge turned down his request. Soon the clerk in the judge's office called.

"Deputy Rivera, he'll see you now."

"I'm on my way."

Rivera's meeting with the judge was brief. He asked a few probing questions but, in the end, the request was approved. The deputy returned to the office, informed the sheriff, and recruited Deputy Sheriff Dave Tibbetts to accompany him in executing the search warrant.

37

RIVERA PARKED IN FRONT of Emiliano Navarro's house, and Tibbetts pulled up behind him. A brand-new ballistics stereo microscope recently acquired by the Sheriff's Office was set up in the lab and a deputy newly trained in its use was standing by. This would be only the second time the department used it in an ongoing case.

There was an excellent chance Navarro had nothing to do with Derek Webster's death, but Rivera was about to treat him like a suspect. All this just a few weeks after his daughter's death. Not a pleasant duty. He looked at Dave Tibbetts, shrugged, and knocked on the door of the Navarro home. After a long wait, the door opened. Navarro looked like he had just gotten out of bed. He was wearing a T-shirt and threadbare khaki shorts. He was barefoot and his hair was disheveled. He looked at Rivera, then Tibbetts, then back at Rivera. He said nothing and waited, his expression blank.

"Sorry to bother you again, Mr. Navarro. May we come in?"

"Uh, sure." He pulled the door open, and the deputies stepped inside.

"I wasn't sure if you'd be home or at work."

"Oh. I took a leave of absence after I lost Lucia. I haven't gone back to work yet. What can I do for you?"

Rivera cleared his throat. "We find it necessary to check any weapons you might own. We're doing this simply to eliminate you as a suspect, thereby making our investigation a little simpler. It narrows down the field of possibilities. The warrant is for your house and vehicle." He handed Navarro the search warrant.

Navarro looked at it, frowned, and handed it back. "Well, whatever, go ahead."

"We'll need to borrow the keys to your vehicle."

He reached into his pocket, extracted the keys, and handed them to Rivera.

"Deputy Tibbetts will do the search. You and I can sit here in the living room and wait." Tibbetts pulled on a pair of Latex gloves, took the keys from Rivera, and went outside. Rivera stayed with Navarro to make sure he didn't slip away. If it became necessary, he could take him back to the Sheriff's Office and formally detain him.

After a few minutes, Tibbetts returned to the house and put the keys on the coffee table. "No weapons in the vehicle," he said to Rivera.

He then began a search of the house. It didn't take long, as the house was small. After a few minutes, he came out of the bedroom holding a 30-06 Remington rifle and a partially filled box of cartridges. "Just this one weapon. I'll be back as soon as I can," he said to Rivera. He exited the house.

Rivera looked at Navarro. He expected him to be irritated, but he sat there on the couch, calm and relaxed. "He'll be back right after the rifle is tested. It shouldn't take long."

For the next hour, Rivera tried to make conversation with Navarro. He asked him about the construction projects he'd worked on and where he'd come from in Mexico. He received mostly nods, grunts, and one-word answers in response. Rivera finally quit asking questions. He thought about telling Navarro about his own life to help pass the time but decided against it. The two men sat there in the quiet of the room, the silence punctuated by the occasional barking of a dog down the street. Rivera looked at his watch, trying to remain patient.

Finally, he heard Tibbetts pull up in front of the house. He stood up and looked outside. Tibbetts seemed to be in a hurry. Rivera stepped outside.

Tibbetts was nodding. "It's a match for the bullet that killed Derek Webster," he said in a low voice. The two deputies entered the house. Navarro was sitting there with a neutral expression on his face. Rivera and Tibbetts sat down.

Rivera read Navarro his rights, and Navarro indicated that he understood them.

"The bullet that killed Derek Webster came from your rifle. Can you explain that?"

"Sure, I can explain it. I shot him."

"You admit it?"

"Damn right. What I did was only fair. My wife Flora died years ago, and Lucia was our only child. With Lucia gone, I no longer have a reason to live. You can lock me up or do whatever you want. I don't care. Whether you found out that I killed him, or you didn't, I was destined to be miserable for the rest of my life. Lucia was my whole life. I have no other relatives except for a few distant cousins back in Mexico. I wanted a life with my daughter and, hopefully someday, lots of grandkids. A full life. When she was taken from me, all that was gone forever."

"But why did you kill Derek Webster? He had nothing to do with Lucia's death."

"You don't know what it was like. Making the funeral arrangements, picking out a coffin, choosing what dress she would wear, deciding on a burial site. And then the funeral itself. It tore my heart out. Lucia was gone, and I was alone. Forever. I cried as I built the roadside memorial in her honor and thought about the peyote that killed her. She wasn't a doper. I suspect she'd never even tried marijuana. But someone was responsible for bringing that peyote into her life. That's when I started visiting you at the sheriff's office. You weren't much help."

"But I told you what happened. The DEA..."

"I know what you told me but look at it from my point of view. I didn't know about the DEA, and it looked like the sheriff's office didn't give a damn. To me, it appeared that nothing was being done to find out who was responsible for killing my girl."

Rivera was silent. He knew the man was right. Maybe he should have told him the DEA was working on the case.

"After several visits to your office, I began to think I'd never get any help from law enforcement. So I decided to take matters into my own hands. I knew the kids Lucia hung around with at school. They used to come to our house to play games and cards. Bill Toliver was one of them. He seemed like a know-it-all type, so I went to him first. I found him at the basketball courts. I asked him who brought the peyote into Lucia's life, but he refused to tell me. 'I'm not a stool pigeon,' he said, acting like a tough guy. Smart aleck. So I roughed him up a bit until he told me about a guy named Jimmy Ventner who lived in Cisco. I was afraid I'd hit Toliver too hard because it took a while before he got up. He had a bloody lip and a swollen eye. I didn't really want to hurt him, but I guess I was a little out of my mind.

"Anyway, I found the Ventner kid by asking around the Cisco community. Skinny kid. He looked kind of like a freak. I got in his face and asked him about the peyote. I had him so scared, he pissed in his pants. He told me right away that the source of the peyote was the Webster Nursery. He said they grew it in the greenhouses."

"So why kill Derek?"

"I did some research on Hal Webster, the owner of the nursery. I thought about killing him for what he'd done to my daughter, but I realized that would only punish him for a brief period. Only for as long as the barrel of a gun was pointed at him and until the trigger was pulled. A very brief period of fear and pain." Navarro was looking past Rivera as he spoke. Now his eyes seemed to have evolved into the eyes of a madman.

"In learning about him, I discovered that, like me, he had an only child. If I killed his child, he would suffer for the rest of his life. Just like me. So I learned about Derek and his drone business. Then one day I followed him into the mountains, approached his position from a small canyon, and shot him dead. Now that sonofabitch Hal Webster can suffer for the rest of his life just like I'm suffering."

Navarro seemed relieved that he'd gotten all that off his chest. He sat there relaxed, with a frightening smile on his face.

Rivera felt like he'd been kicked in the stomach. He was almost speechless. He looked at Dave Tibbetts who was staring back at him with a look of disbelief. Rivera locked eyes with Navarro.

"Mr. Navarro, Hal Webster knew nothing about the peyote in his greenhouse. One of his employees was growing it there in secret. You killed Derek Webster when neither him nor his father had anything to do with the peyote."

Navarro's jaw slowly dropped, and the blood seemed to drain from his face. "You mean I killed the man's only child by mistake?"

Rivera pushed himself out of his chair. "That's right."

Navarro lowered his head and covered his face with his hands. "Oh, God. Dear, dear God. What have I done?"

Rivera placed him under arrest and cuffed his hands behind his back. He led him to his vehicle and placed him in the back seat. Driving back to the sheriff's building, he thought about how foolish revenge is. Now Navarro will spend the rest of his life in anguish not only because of the loss of his daughter but also because of the knowledge that he cast the same fate upon an innocent man.

38

AFTER BOOKING THE PRISONER and locking him in a jail cell, Rivera went to Sheriff Anderson's office to bring her up to date. He felt mentally exhausted. "You're not going to believe what I'm about to tell you."

"Tell me."

"Emiliano Navarro murdered Derek Webster."

"What? Are you sure?"

"He made a full confession in front of me and Dave Tibbetts. He did it freely and openly, almost as easily as if we were talking about the weather."

"What on earth was his reason for killing Derek Webster?"

"It's the strangest motive I've ever run across. I've never heard of anything like it." Rivera explained how Navarro was able to narrow down the source of the peyote to the Webster Nursery, how he learned that Hal Webster had an only child, and how he reasoned that exacting his revenge by killing Hal wouldn't be nearly as strong and long-lasting a punishment as killing his son Derek.

Killing Hal would cause him pain for a few seconds, but killing his son would cause him pain for life."

"Good Lord. What a dreadful state of mind."

"I think he was depressed and emotionally irrational. His wife was gone and so was Lucia. He must have felt like he had nothing to live for."

"I met him once during his first visit here after Lucia's accident. He seemed like a gentleman, a normal citizen, not a man who could commit murder."

"Yeah. He was a gentleman at first, but as his frustration with law enforcement grew, I guess he became bitter and completely lost it. I'm no psychologist, but I'd say he quietly went mad. In a way, he was also a victim. If we had told him the DEA was handling the investigation, he might not have gone off the deep end and killed Derek. I think frustration with the law enforcement system was partly to blame for his actions. To tell you the truth, I feel a certain amount of guilt myself."

"Well, don't. We're obligated to cooperate with other law enforcement agencies, and that includes the DEA."

She thought for a long moment. "Don't we have a case against Richardson and Ventner too? And maybe Bill Toliver and the rest of those kids who tried the peyote?"

"I've thought about that. The kids who tried it will probably never try it again. It's unlikely they'll ever get the opportunity. So my advice is to let me talk to each one of them, with their parents present, about the dangers of experimenting with illicit drugs. Bill Toliver or Abigail

Nolan can give me the names of the others who tried it. That's probably the best we can do for the community. Leaving those kids with a police record will damage their futures and probably accomplish nothing."

"I agree. What about Richardson and Ventner?"

"Richardson was not a user, nor did he sell the peyote. His interest was strictly botanical. He's a collector of different kinds of cactus. He gave some cuttings to Ventner, a fellow member of the Moab Succulent Club, believing Ventner was going to plant them, not use them as a hallucinogenic. So I don't see the point of arresting Richardson. He's a good citizen of the community. I doubt he'll ever see peyote again in his lifetime. I think he's learned his lesson, but to be sure, I suggest we detain him, bring him to your office, and have a discussion along the lines of whether to place him under arrest. Long discussion, then you decide to take no action."

"You mean frighten him."

"Right. That'll teach him a lesson he won't soon forget and at the same time won't damage his future by giving him a police record. Again, I think that's the best thing we can do for the community."

Anderson nodded. "Okay, we'll try it your way. This would never work in a big city, but for a small town like Moab, I think that's a sensible approach. Now, what about Ventner?"

"Ventner is a different case. An unusual case. I like the kid. He doesn't seem like a menace to anyone. He's just, well, different. He would love to be a Navajo. He's building a hogan behind his brother's house in Cisco, right next to the brush arbor and sweat lodge he built. He wears his hair long, all the way down his back, and wears face paint. He's trying to join the Native American Church and hopes to someday be accepted. He's a genuinely good person but he did distribute peyote buttons to those U.S.U. kids, and that led directly to Lucia Navarro's death."

"So we prosecute?"

"With regard to prosecuting him, I may have blown that possibility. I didn't Mirandize him before he admitted to distributing peyote to his friends. I needed information from him about his source, which he freely gave me. There was probably a better way to handle all that."

"If you'd read him his rights before questioning him, you might have spooked him into remaining silent. Then you would never have been able to trace Derek's murder to Emiliano Navarro. Navarro would still be free as a bird. So I don't think you should have any regrets."

"It's probably all moot, anyway. Jimmy's brother told me Jimmy has late-stage glioblastoma. It's some kind of brain tumor. I asked Dr. Pudge Devlin about it. He said chances of survival are slim, probably less than a year."

"So we should let the prosecution of Ventner slide?"

"I think that makes sense. But I think we should give him the same treatment as Richardson. Bring him in and frighten him."

"Okay, that's settled, now what do we do with the peyote in the evidence locker?"

Rivera chuckled. "We could give it to Masters next time he's in town."

Anderson grinned. "By the way, he called this morning. The DEA followed up on that Tommy Redhorse lead you gave them. Turns out Redhorse, his uncle, and some cousins were involved in a peyote racket on the rez. They acquired it legally from *peyoteros*, sold some to the Native American Church legally, and siphoned off the rest to sell on the black market. The feds made a lot of arrests, both on and off the rez. He said to tell you he sends his regards."

Rivera smiled. "Sounds like I've got a new friend."

He returned to his office, closed the door, and fell heavily into his chair. He was mentally exhausted, having seen yet another example of the evil the human race was capable of. He turned on his computer and completed his final case report which, for him, was almost like reliving the investigation with all of its associated stress, frustration, and disappointment in humanity. He felt no sense of victory, no measure of achievement. His work was done, but he knew his numbness of spirit would linger for a long while. It always did to varying degrees, but this case, because of the vile nature of Navarro's motive, would be worse than the others.

He was glad Gloria would be home soon.

39

THE FOLLOWING DAY was mild and sunny, and there was hardly a cloud in the sky. Rivera was having a late lunch with Chris Carey. They sat at one of the outside tables at La Jacaranda Mexican Restaurant, protected from the sun by a dark green awning. Their table was nestled in the far corner, far enough from the other patrons so that if they spoke softly, they wouldn't be overheard. Carey was eagerly probing Rivera for the details of the Derek Webster murder case. Rivera went through it all, covering each step of the investigation in detail. At the end, he thanked Carey for his help.

"Your interview with Bill Toliver was a key in breaking the case."

"Always glad to help."

"By the way, those bruises on Toliver's face weren't from playing basketball. Emiliano Navarro roughed him up until he named the person who had introduced peyote into his daughter's life."

"I guess Bill was too embarrassed to tell me about that."

Rich Curtin

"Probably. A young macho guy wouldn't want people to know he'd been whipped by a middle-aged man, although Navarro looked like he was all muscle."

"So, case closed," said Carey.

"Case closed. And two dreams shattered. Navarro loses his daughter and goes to prison with his dreams of becoming a grandfather dashed. He'll have the rest of his life to think about what he's done. And Hal Webster goes through life without Derek or his hoped-for grandchildren. Both dreams crushed. It's very sad."

"There is one bright side to this, though. I drove out to the nursery this morning to visit Hal and give him my condolences. Turns out that Evelyn Ellwood, Derek's girlfriend, is pregnant with Derek's child. She's moving out to the nursery to live in the cabin out there. Hal said he would support her financially and help raise the child. So, Hal will have a grandchild after all."

Rivera smiled. "I hadn't heard that. That's great news."

"Anything new on the wolves?"

"Nothing new, but I believe they're here to stay. We'll just have to get used to our new neighbors." Rivera looked at his watch. "Time for me to leave. I'm headed for the airport to pick up Gloria."

Rivera paid the tab, thanked Carey one last time, and walked to his vehicle. He was glad Gloria's BLM training program had ended, and their long separation was over. Maybe this evening he would take her to Pasta Jay's for dinner. She loved the chicken parmesan they served. That and a bottle of Chianti would be perfect for celebrating her homecoming.

As he drove toward the small Moab airport 18 miles to the north, the lives of Emiliano Navarro and Hal Webster occupied his thoughts. When their children Lucia and Derek were born, the two men had no idea of the grief and pain awaiting them in the years ahead. As he thought about each man losing his only child, the risks associated with having children returned to the focus of his thinking. He dwelled on that as he drove, then spotted the airport up ahead on the left.

Soon he would have Gloria back in his arms. He recalled the last three telephone conversations they had. She seemed so happy while they were talking. He imagined she was having fun sharing time with the other BLM trainees, learning about each other, and hearing the stories of their lives. Dinner in the evenings, he thought. Maybe a drink with dinner. As he thought about all that, he began to resent that she had such a good time without him. He pushed that thought away.

He parked, walked to the small waiting room, and sat down. He liked the Moab airport. It lacked the crowds, bustle, and noise of larger airports. He didn't have to wait long. The Contour Airlines Embraer aircraft was right on time. He stood by the window and watched as the passengers deplaned. Soon he spotted Gloria. She produced a big smile and waved when she saw him waiting there. She rushed through the open door into his arms.

"Manny, I'm so happy. I've known for a whole week, but I didn't want to tell you over the telephone. I wanted you holding me."

"Tell me what?"

"Manny, I'm pregnant. We're going to have a baby."

Rivera's spirits soared. He was thrilled. He held Gloria tight in his arms and kissed her. And now he understood why she sounded so happy on the phone. As he stood there holding her, the risks of having children and the unforeseen perils that befell Hal Webster and Emiliano Navarro flashed in his mind for an instant, but he rejected them out of hand. After all, he'd be there to love and protect his child.

AUTHOR'S NOTE

For purposes of crafting this fictional story, I took some liberties with the regulations that govern hunting in Utah. In actual fact, the Utah Division of Wildlife Resources prohibits using drones in the taking of protected wildlife including elk, as such high-tech tracking and hunting would put the animals at a significant disadvantage. I used a certain amount of literary license in this respect.